# A HOSTILE ATTITUDE

"What do you think you're doing to that animal?" George looked at Lisa, Carole, and Stevie and frowned. "Are these girls professional trainers? Are they accustomed to working with valuable equine actors?"

"They are my guests, George," Skye said reasonably. "They are here at my invitation."

"And they are leaving at *my* invitation!" said George, tapping his riding crop against the side of his boot.

"I think you're being unfair, George," protested Skye. "These girls are expert horsewomen. Far better riders than I am."

"It wouldn't take much to be a better rider than you, Ransom." George's upper lip curled in a snarl.

For an instant, Skye's fists clenched in anger, then he turned and smiled at the girls.

"I'm sorry you had to see the ugly side of filmmaking," he apologized loudly. "Let's go back to my trailer. The atmosphere is a lot friendlier there!"

*Other books you will enjoy*

CAMY BAKER'S HOW TO BE POPULAR
IN THE SIXTH GRADE by Camy Baker

CAMY BAKER'S LOVE YOU LIKE A SISTER
by Camy Baker

ANNE OF GREEN GABLES by L. M. Montgomery

HORSE CRAZY (The Saddle Club #1) by Bonnie Bryant

AMY, NUMBER SEVEN (Replica #1) by Marilyn Kaye

PURSUING AMY (Replica #2) by Marilyn Kaye

THE CASE OF THE MISSING MARBLES
AND THE CASE OF THE RISING MOON
(The Adventures of Shirley Holmes) by John Whitman

# the SADDLE CLUB

# STARTING GATE

## BONNIE BRYANT

A SKYLARK BOOK
NEW YORK · TORONTO · LONDON · SYDNEY · AUCKLAND

Special thanks to Sir "B" Farms
and Laura and Vinny Marino

RL: 5, ages 009–012

STARTING GATE
A Bantam Skylark Book / March 2000

ISBN: 0-553-48695-0

Published simultaneously in the United States and Canada

Bantam Skylark is an imprint of Random House Children's Books. SKY-
LARK BOOK, BANTAM BOOKS, and the rooster colophon are registered
trademarks of Random House, Inc., Bantam Books, 1540 Broadway,
New York, New York 10036.

PRINTED IN THE UNITED STATES OF AMERICA
OPM       10  9  8  7  6  5  4  3  2  1

I would like to express my special thanks
to Sallie Bissell for her
help in the writing of this book.

This book belongs to

Jillian Gisbey

1

"I'M SUPPOSED TO take these horses where?" The lanky young man with the long blond ponytail scratched his head as he leaned against the huge red In-Transit horse trailer.

"Ashford Farms, California," gushed Stevie Lake. "The National Pony Club Competition. In five days Carole and Lisa and I are riding in it. We all belong to The Saddle Club. Veronica's riding in it, too, but she's not a member of The Saddle Club. Max and Deborah and Maxi are going, too, but they're not riding. Max is too old, and, well, Maxi, she's only a baby."

"Huh?" The young man frowned. Stevie realized he was far from absorbing the torrent of words that

1

were spilling from her mouth. The look on his face was total confusion.

"California," Stevie repeated. "A group of us from Pine Hollow are riding in the Pony Club competition there."

"California?" The young man stared at her as if he'd never heard of California before.

"Yes!" Stevie cried, almost dancing with excitement. "California! You know. Movie stars. Orange groves. Giant redwood trees."

"California?" he repeated again, his eyes glazing over.

"Ca-li-for-nia." Veronica diAngelo walked over to the man and spoke slowly, as if she were addressing some alien from outer space. "The only state that stands between Nevada and the Pacific Ocean."

The young man turned and blinked. "Really?"

"Don't confuse him with geography, Veronica," Lisa Atwood suggested in a whisper.

That was when Mrs. Reg, who managed Pine Hollow Stables for her son, Max, tuned in to their conversation. "Why not show him on the map, girls?" she said as she checked through a stack of official-looking Pony Club papers.

Veronica, Stevie, and Lisa unfolded the map that the young man had been clutching in his hand and spread it out on the gleaming hood of the red truck.

"Here." Stevie squinted in the bright sun and pointed to a small dot on the right edge of the map. "Here's where we are: Willow Creek, Virginia. You're supposed to drive our horses over here"—she slowly moved her finger all the way across the map—"to Ashford Farms, just outside Los Angeles, California."

For a moment no one breathed as the young man's gaze followed Stevie's finger. "Okay," he finally said. "Cool. You want me to drive here." He poked one finger down in the middle of California.

"Right." Everyone sighed with relief.

"But where are the horses?"

Everyone groaned.

"There!" Stevie cried, pointing toward the van. "You're taking Prancer and Danny and Starlight and Belle, our four horses. Carole and Max are loading them into your van now!"

"Oh!" The young man suddenly grinned. "Those horses. I wondered where they were going!"

At that, Mrs. Reg glared at the young man and gathered up her papers. "I'm calling the In-Transit people right this minute," she announced, stomping off toward the barn. "Every April they promise me they'll send somebody out here who can drive horses and today we wind up with a driver who can't tell a horse from a hedgehog!"

Everyone watched in awkward silence as Mrs. Reg disappeared into the barn.

"I don't know what she's so upset about," the driver sighed. "I mean, like, I haven't done anything wrong."

"Have you ever driven horses before?" Stevie asked more gently.

"Sure I have," he replied, smoothing his stringy hair back behind his ears. "I used to drive Captain Gizmo's Magic Pony Ride all over this county."

Stevie and Lisa exchanged quick glances of terror. It was nerve-racking enough to be entering a national competition all the way on the other side of the country, but to entrust the horses they loved best in the world to someone whose only previous experience seemed to be driving Captain Gizmo's Magic Pony Ride was almost too much.

"Maybe this was not such a great idea," Stevie whispered in Lisa's ear. "Maybe we should all just compete in the show next year, when it will be closer to home."

"Wait," Lisa whispered back, giving Stevie a quick wink as she turned to the driver. "Since you've worked with Captain Gizmo, you must know that horses aren't like regular cargo. You've got to take time to water and feed them."

"Yeah. I know all about horses. You can't let them get too hot or they'll throw up or something." The young man put his cap on and began to climb into the cab of the In-Transit truck. "Well, I'm ready. California, here we come!"

"Wait!" cried Lisa. "We haven't loaded our tack trunks!"

"Or the feeding instructions," added Stevie.

"Or Danny!" Veronica added, watching as Max and Carole led the big gray Thoroughbred out of the barn and up to the loading ramp.

"But I've got a schedule to keep—" the young man began.

"Not without Danny and the rest of our stuff, you don't," Stevie snapped, her patience wearing thin. "You just stand there and don't move until everything gets loaded!"

Stevie and Lisa kept one eye on the driver while Carole loaded Danny, then Max and Red O'Malley pushed three tack trunks into the enormous trailer.

"Say, while we're standing here, let me give you these pills for my horse," Veronica chirped to the driver as she dug out a small bottle of green capsules from the pocket of her jeans.

"Which one is yours?" the driver asked, frowning at the pills.

"The big gray gelding they just loaded. You should check on him every half hour or so. He's a Thoroughbred and they're notorious about going crazy on road trips."

"I don't know about this . . ." The driver swallowed hard.

"He's skittish," Veronica continued. "He's got these incredible bloodlines—"

Stevie interrupted her with a snort. "Veronica, the last time we trucked Danny to a show we practically had to wake him up to lead him off the trailer. He's not a problem on the road at all." She sighed at Veronica's need for special attention even from this idiot truck driver. "Why don't you wait until Danny's been on the van for at least five minutes before you have the driver start medicating him?"

"Oh, all right," sighed Veronica, putting the medicine back in her pocket. "It's just such a hot day for early April, and all we're doing is standing around wasting time."

"Yeah," grumbled the driver. "I need to get on the road right away. By the way, how far is it to California?"

Stevie and Lisa looked at each other as if they might cry. "Four days," Stevie croaked, a hard lump of fear now lodged firmly in her throat. "You need to have our horses there by Thursday."

"No problem," chuckled the driver. "I once drove Captain Gizmo's magic ponies from Willow Creek to English Mountain in fifteen minutes. I know I can get these four horses to California by Thursday."

Just then Max and Carole jumped down from the

trailer. "Okay," Max said. "We're all set. The horses are in good shape, listening to Mozart, thanks to Carole's cassette player. Everything in order here?"

"No." Stevie crossed her arms over her chest. "We're about as far from being in order as we can get." She turned and looked at Max. She hated to be rude, but the safety of their horses was at stake. "Max," she said softly, hoping she sounded diplomatic, "I don't know if this driver has the experience we need to get our horses to California."

"Oh?" Max turned and studied the driver, his blue eyes flashing with concern. "You ever haul show horses before, buddy?"

"Captain Gizmo's Magic Pony Ride," the young man said proudly just as Mrs. Reg hurried up from the barn.

"Okay, everybody. I just talked to the In-Transit people," she announced, little wisps of gray hair curling around her flushed face. "Seems the driver who was supposed to pick up these horses broke his leg yesterday. This is Darrell, the substitute driver."

"And?" Max's brows wrinkled in a frown.

"And Darrell has driven both cows and horses before, but more importantly, he's scheduled to meet the certified horse transport expert in Richmond, which isn't far away at all."

Darrell nodded. "I drive that route at least twice a week. That's where I thought I was supposed to take these horses. You guys were the ones who started jabbering about California."

Everyone stopped talking and looked at Stevie.

"Well, okay." She shrugged apologetically. "Maybe I did jabber about California a little bit. I didn't mean to confuse any drivers, though."

"Okay," said Max. "Now that we're all clear on our destination, let's get going."

"Here. Let me give you Danny's pills now." Veronica once again waved the bottle of pills in Darrell's face.

"For Pete's sake, Veronica," said Stevie. "Don't distract him before he can even get the gate locked on the trailer. Give me the pills and I'll give them to him later—after we're sure he's leaving with everything he's supposed to take."

"You won't forget? Traveling makes Danny crazy."

"Veronica, you're what makes Danny crazy, not taking a trip to California." Stevie took the pills from Veronica. "But I'll give them to Darrell, just to be sure."

"Thanks." Veronica wiped her forehead with the back of her hand. "I think I need to go back in the office where it's cool. I'm feeling a little faint."

"Fine," muttered Stevie, turning her attention back to the van. "Just faint somewhere out of the way."

Veronica glared at Stevie, but then turned and hurried to Mrs. Reg's air-conditioned office. Stevie tossed Danny's tranquilizers into her backpack while Max went over a copy of all the horses' medical forms with Darrell.

"Hey, Stevie," Lisa called down from the loading ramp. "Don't you want to kiss Belle good-bye?"

"Of course I do!" Stevie hurried up the ramp and into the van, where she was relieved to see all the horses munching hay inside surprisingly roomy stalls. Just as Max had said, soothing violin music was floating from Carole's tape player. Maybe this wasn't going to be so bad after all.

"Gosh," she said as she gave Belle a long good-bye scratch behind her ears. "This looks great. These guys look more comfortable than we'll be on the airplane!"

"I know," agreed Lisa. "Even if they do have a nitwit for a driver, at least they've got a wonderful traveling stable!"

"Come on, girls!" Max's voice echoed from the ground. "All two-legged personnel need to disembark. Darrell wants to get rolling!"

They bid their horses good-bye, then Darrell locked the back of the van and climbed into the cab. The huge engine started with a growl and all the running lights of the trailer came on. Slowly he began to drive down the driveway.

"See you in California!" he yelled at the three girls, laughing as he waved his cap out the window.

Stevie, Carole, and Lisa watched, waving, until the trailer crossed a little bridge and the van's taillights disappeared around a curve.

"Thank heavens that's over," sighed Mrs. Reg, fanning herself with an old saddle pad.

"Mrs. Reg, do you really think that guy is okay?" Stevie asked worriedly. "I mean, he seemed incredibly dumb. Maybe we should have gotten some kind of special alarm to put on the back of the trailer."

"Like what, Stevie?" laughed Lisa. "A dumb alarm?"

"I don't know. A wrong turn alarm. A wrong state alarm." Stevie's hair seemed to stand on end. "Maybe even a wrong country alarm. He might take our horses to Mexico!"

"Oh, Stevie, he's all right. He just got confused. We were all running around like chickens with our heads cut off." Mrs. Reg gave her a kind smile. "Anyway, he's only driving to Richmond. There an older, more reliable driver will take over."

"That worries me even more," admitted Stevie. "Who knows how many total strangers are going to be driving our precious horses all over the country?"

Mrs. Reg gave Stevie a quick hug. "Stevie, this is a reputable company, and they're bonded and insured. I'm sure there won't be any more problems."

"Mrs. Reg is right, Stevie," said Lisa. "Anyway, whoever drives the truck has excellent directions to Ashford Farms."

"It's not Ashford Farms I'm worried about," replied Stevie. "I'm afraid they won't be able to find California!"

"Oh, Stevie." Carole laughed. "Why don't we go over to TD's and calm down with a Saddle Club meeting?"

"Good idea," said Lisa. "There's nothing left to do here, anyway, except miss our horses. And we've got lots to talk about, like our trip!"

"Well, all right," Stevie agreed reluctantly, giving a final worried glance to the small cloud of dust the trailer had left behind.

A FEW MINUTES later The Saddle Club settled into their regular booth at TD's, the local ice-cream shop where the girls held many of their meetings. They had formed The Saddle Club a while back, when they had discovered they had something in common: They were all totally crazy about horses. So far the club had three regular members—Stevie, Lisa, and Carole—and several out-of-town members. The only rules were that members had to love horses and help each other out whenever possible.

"What are you going to have today, girls?" asked their usual waitress.

"A small chocolate malt for me, please," said Lisa.

"Me too," added Carole.

The waitress scribbled on her pad, then waited for Stevie to decide.

"I'd like a lime and orange sherbet sundae with fudge sauce and marshmallows, please," said Stevie, smiling.

"Is that with marshmallow cream or just regular marshmallows?" the waitress asked with a shudder.

"Uh, marshmallow cream today," Stevie replied.

"Coming up," the waitress said, shaking her head.

"And mint chips."

"Coming up."

"Oh, and don't forget the cherry."

"Who could?"

"Thanks." Stevie watched as the waitress took their order to the counter, then she turned to her friends, her eyes wide with excitement.

"Can you believe that in less than a week we're actually going to be competing in a Pony Club competition in California?"

"No," said Carole, tossing her long dark hair. "But then I can't believe that Veronica and I are entered in the same hunter-jumper class. Imagine traveling three thousand miles to team up with the snootiest, most spoiled rider at Pine Hollow!"

"Oh, you'll see lots of other riders there besides

Veronica, Carole," Lisa reminded her. "I know I'll see lots of great riding in my equitation class."

"And I'll be competing against some wonderful dressage riders," Stevie added. "I'm just glad all four of us will be competing as a team in the mounted games."

"The Saddle Club should do great," said Carole. "I just hope Veronica cooperates."

"She probably won't, but what else is new?" Stevie grinned as the waitress handed her a bowl of pastel-colored ice cream covered with dark brown sauce, white goo, bright green chips, and the promised red cherry.

"I just hope we haven't forgotten anything," said Lisa as she took a swallow of chocolate malt.

"Did you get suntan lotion for the wonderful tan you'll get?" asked Carole.

Lisa nodded. "My mother already packed it."

"Did you get an autograph book for the thousands of movie stars we'll see?" asked Stevie.

Lisa nodded again. "I'm bringing something even more wonderful than that."

"What?" Stevie and Carole asked together.

"I've got Skye Ransom's phone number. I read in a fan magazine that he's filming a movie about race-horses. Maybe when he's not shooting, he can come and watch us compete."

"Wow," said Stevie. "That would be great. We haven't seen Skye in a long time."

"Maybe we could go visit him when we're not competing, too," said Carole. "It would be fun to be on a movie set with him again."

"I think this is going to be one of our greatest trips of all time!" said Stevie.

"Me too," agreed Carole. "I only hope our horses enjoy it half as much as we will!"

2

"Look down there, Stevie!" Carole teased. "It looks like Darrell and our horses!"

Stevie shifted little Maxi Regnery to her left knee and leaned across Carole's seat. Thousands of feet below them, on a thin gray ribbon of highway, Stevie saw what looked like a bright red horse trailer, crawling along like an ant.

"You really think so?" Stevie lifted one eyebrow in curiosity.

"No." Carole laughed and shook her head. "Even if Darrell were the best horse driver in the world, I don't think he could possibly have driven our horses this far west."

"Yeah, Stevie," said Lisa from the aisle seat.

15

"We've already begun our descent to L.A. Darrell's probably still trying to figure out how to get to Richmond."

"Don't say that, you guys!" Stevie cried. "If our horses don't show up, then this whole trip will be a total waste!"

"Calm down, Stevie," said Carole. "We're just kidding. Mrs. Reg assured us that Darrell would turn the truck over to a more experienced driver in Richmond. Our horses are probably rolling through Arkansas right now, munching hay and listening to Mozart."

"Yeeoowww!" Stevie jumped as Maxi chomped down on one of her fingers. "And little Maxi is up here, munching on me!"

"Sorry, Stevie." Deborah Regnery leaned up from the seat behind Stevie, where she was sitting. She clapped her hands and held out her arms for Maxi. "I should have warned you—she's cutting teeth and chewing on everything. I'll buckle her into her seat now."

"No problem." Stevie laughed, rubbing the four small tooth marks on her finger. "Just as long as she doesn't act like Belle and mistake me for a carrot!"

The plane gave a small lurch, and the pilot's voice came over the intercom. "Ladies and gentlemen, please keep your seat belts fastened for our final approach to Los Angeles International Airport. We

16

should be landing in approximately fifteen minutes. Currently, the weather in Los Angeles is clear and seventy-eight degrees. We've enjoyed having you on this flight, and hope you'll fly with us again soon."

"California, here we come!" Stevie grinned at her friends as they all tightened their seat belts and prepared to land.

A little while later all seven of them hurried through the huge Los Angeles airport, trying to get to the right baggage carousel. Max had Maxi in a carrier on his back, and the little girl's eyes popped at the activity swirling around them. All sorts of people hurried past—bearded men in turbans, three women dressed in bright yellow saris, two men wearing black cowboy hats and carrying big guitar cases. Lots of different languages and accents floated through the air.

"This is nuts," whispered Stevie as a man carrying a big silver vulture-shaped kite almost ran into a flight attendant.

"No." Carole laughed. "This is California. Keep your eyes peeled. We might see somebody famous."

Peering curiously at everyone who wore sunglasses, they hurried down a long corridor until Max pointed them to the carousel where their luggage would be unloaded.

"Whew!" gasped Deborah, taking Maxi in her arms. "That was quite a stroll."

"You got that right." Max checked his boarding

pass to make sure they were in the correct place. "How many bags are we waiting for?"

"One for me," said Stevie.

"One for each of us," added Lisa and Carole.

"I've got three," replied Veronica, carelessly shrugging her shoulders.

"Well, we may as well make ourselves comfortable." Max sighed. "This will probably take a while."

The girls sat down and waited for their luggage to roll onto the carousel. "Let's make some plans," said Lisa, leaning back in her seat. "Today is Tuesday. We've got two whole days to enjoy California before the horses get here. What should we do?"

"We could go and watch some of the other events at the rally." Carole glanced at her watch. "It started fifteen minutes ago."

"That would be fun," agreed Stevie. "But we'll be spending most of the weekend there already. It might be cool to do some other California-type things until the horses get here."

"Like go to Disneyland?" asked Lisa, waving back at Maxi, who was playing peekaboo from her mother's arms.

"Yes. And Knott's Berry Farm," Stevie suggested. "Both those places are lots of fun."

"And don't forget the La Brea Tar Pits," added Carole.

"Oh, who would possibly want to see a bunch of old fossils when you can go shopping?" sneered Veronica. "My mother told me there are some wonderful new shops on Rodeo Drive."

"I don't think my budget will allow shopping on Rodeo Drive," Lisa answered with a sigh.

"Mine won't, either," said Stevie. "Anyway, shopping sounds like a waste of perfectly good California sunshine."

"Look!" Carole cried, her brown eyes wide. "Do you see what I see?" She pointed to the other side of the baggage carousel, where a tall, white-haired man in a blue blazer was holding a sign that had THE SADDLE CLUB printed on it in bright red letters.

Stevie shook her head. "I must be having an attack of jet lag. I could almost swear that says 'The Saddle Club.'"

Lisa looked at the sign. "It does say 'The Saddle Club.' I just had my eyes checked last month, and my vision's twenty-twenty."

Stevie looked at her friends. "Do you think Skye could have found out when our plane was landing and sent someone to meet us?"

Carole shrugged, but Lisa giggled. "I think all he had to do was read the e-mail I sent him!"

"Lisa!" Carole cried. "Why didn't you tell us?"

"I don't know." Lisa grinned. "I guess I wanted it

19

to be a surprise. Also, I wasn't sure how often Skye checked his e-mail when he's making a movie."

"Well, go over and tell that guy we're The Saddle Club," Stevie said. "Who knows what Skye might have in mind?"

"Okay." Lisa left her purse with Stevie and Carole and walked over to the dignified-looking man. They chatted for a few minutes, then they both walked back to the baggage carousel.

"Everybody, this is Stephan," said Lisa. "Skye's chauffeur."

"How do you do." Stephan smiled at the girls and shook hands with Max and Deborah. "I have strict orders from Mr. Ransom that I am to drive you all to your hotel."

"No kidding?" Pleasantly surprised, Max looked at the girls.

"That's correct." Stephan smiled again and handed Lisa a sheet of monogrammed Skye Ransom stationery. "In fact, Mr. Ransom insists that you call him as soon as you get your riding jackets hung up. That's the way he put it."

Lisa looked at the phone number written on the piece of paper. "Cool. Is this where he's making his new movie?"

Stephan nodded. "That number connects you with Mr. Ransom's private trailer." He stopped speaking and looked over as the first suitcases began to appear

20

on the carousel. "I believe your luggage may have arrived."

The girls jumped up and ran over to the carousel. A few moments later they all met up again, each carrying one suitcase, except for Veronica, who was struggling with two large bags. Stephan wrestled with her third one, a boxy thing that could have held a small piano.

"Is this everything?" Stephan asked, beads of sweat breaking out on his forehead.

"That's all *my* things," Veronica said archly.

"Well." Stephan tried to smile as he lugged Veronica's bag toward the door. "Right this way, then."

They followed Stephan out into the warm California sunshine to a special reserved parking area close to the terminal entrance. At the far end of a line of cars stood a huge black limousine. Stephan led them to it, then with a click of a single button on his key ring, all four doors and the trunk opened at once.

"Wow!" cried Stevie as she peered into the huge car. It had dark blue sofas instead of seats, a TV, and a midget refrigerator fully stocked with fruit juice, sodas, and fancy bottled water. "This car is bigger than my room back home!"

Stephan grinned. "Mr. Ransom instructed me to bring the biggest car possible. He said you might be bringing a horse or two with you!"

"Not on the plane," laughed Deborah. "But we

brought Maxi instead. She covers enough territory for a herd of horses."

The girls helped Stephan load their bags into the enormous trunk, then everyone settled back into the velvety seats of the car. Maxi crawled from lap to lap, content to turn the TV set on and off and play with all the shiny buttons.

Stephan smoothly steered the huge car out on to the freeway, and they were on their way to the hotel.

"Stephan, can you tell us more about the movie Skye's making right now?" Lisa leaned forward on the plush sofa.

"Uh, it's something about horses and racetracks, I believe." Stephan's voice was calm, but the girls noticed his troubled frown in the rearview mirror.

"That sounds like something Skye would be perfect for." Carole smiled at the memory of teaching Skye how to ride so long ago in New York.

"It does, doesn't it?" Stephan agreed. "Too bad it's turned out to be such a challenge."

"A challenge?" Stevie frowned. Skye had developed into a good rider—acting in a movie about racehorses should be a piece of cake for him.

Stephan gave a small shrug. "I suppose some roles that look easy in the script turn out to be a lot more difficult once the cameras start rolling."

Stevie shared a mystified glance with Lisa and

Carole. Of all people, Skye Ransom shouldn't be having difficulty with a horseback riding role! Maybe they would have to give him some make-up lessons while they were there.

After a few minutes, they pulled up in the courtyard of a fancy hotel. Palm trees grew around a huge swimming pool, and nearby, people in crisp white outfits played croquet.

"Right this way," the hotel doorman said as he held their doors open. Stephan unloaded the limo while the Easterners checked in at the front desk. Soon they were in their rooms—Lisa, Stevie, and Carole all in one big room; Max, Deborah, and Maxi in another. Veronica had insisted on having a private room.

"I need to relax," Veronica said as she unlocked the door to her room, which was next to The Saddle Club's. "Riding in that limo in all that traffic was unnerving."

"Fine, Veronica," said Carole. "We'll be in our room, unpacking."

By the time Carole closed the door, Stevie and Lisa already had their suitcases open.

"Okay," said Lisa, carefully unfolding her riding jacket. "You guys can witness this. I'm doing exactly what Skye asked: calling as soon as I hang up my jacket."

23

Carole and Stevie watched as Lisa put her jacket in the closet, then pick up the telephone and dial the number written on Skye's stationery.

"Skye?" Lisa said, grinning as the famous, familiar voice came over the line. "Hi. It's Lisa Atwood."

"And Stevie and Carole," Stevie called with a laugh.

"Thank heaven it's you!" Skye sounded so relieved that Lisa frowned.

"Is everything okay?" Lisa sat down on the edge of the bed between Stevie and Carole.

"No," replied Skye, his voice worried and nervous. "Everything is definitely not okay. I really need you. Can you guys come over here? Like right now?"

"Well, I guess so," Lisa said. "Where is here?"

"We're on location at Ashford Racetrack," Skye explained over some static.

Lisa frowned. "Is that near Ashford Farms? Where the Pony Club meet is?"

"I don't know about any Pony Club meet, but Ashford Racetrack is about two miles away from something called Ashford Farms," said Skye.

"Okay," Lisa said. "We'll have to check it out with Max, but I don't see why we can't come right over."

"Great!" replied Skye. "It's a closed set, but I've left your names at the front gate. You shouldn't have any trouble getting in."

"Okay, then. We'll see you in a little while."

"Super. Just hurry, though!"

She hung up the phone, a puzzled frown on her face.

"What's going on?" asked Carole.

Lisa shrugged. "I don't know. Skye sounded very mysterious—and very worried. All he said was that he needed to see us immediately, and to please hurry over. He's left our names at the front gate."

"Gosh." Stevie's eyes grew wide. "Maybe he needs some extra advice on riding." She leaped off the bed. "Maybe he needs us to be technical advisers on this film! I can see our names on the big screen now!"

"I think we'd better ask Max if we can go, first, Stevie," Carole laughed. "Then we can worry about who gets top billing in Skye's movie."

"Okay, okay," agreed Stevie.

They hurried to the room across the hall, where the door was already ajar. Veronica was standing beside the TV set, complaining to Max and Deborah that her bed was lumpy and uncomfortable.

"Hi, guys!" Max looked glad to see them as they trooped into the room. "We were just wondering if you'd like to go to Disneyland with us and take Maxi on the teacup ride."

Lisa glanced at Stevie and Carole. "Actually, Max, we were wondering if we could do something a little different. We just called Skye, and he really needs our help."

25

Max frowned. "What kind of help?"

"We're not sure. All we know is that he's making a movie at Ashford Racetrack and wants us to come see him immediately."

"A real movie set? That sounds a lot more interesting than Disneyland," Veronica cooed hopefully.

"Well, it would be, except that it's a closed set and Skye's only put our three names on the guest list," Lisa explained, hoping this wouldn't hurt Max's and Deborah's feelings.

Max smiled. "Would Skye just happen to have that same limo waiting outside for you?"

The girls ran to the window and looked out. Stephan was standing there, chatting with the hotel doorman, the long black limo stretched out behind him.

"I guess so," Lisa said, amazed that someone would actually have a car waiting to drive them somewhere.

"Well, I guess you'd better go, then, if Skye needs your help that badly," said Max. "Veronica can come with us and take Maxi on the teacup ride."

Veronica made a small noise at the back of her throat. Everyone turned and stared at her. She looked pea green with envy, but there was nothing anyone could do. Her name was not on the guest list, and Hollywood studios were notorious about keeping unwanted people off their sets.

"Then I guess we'll see you guys later," said Lisa. "I hope all of you have a good time at Disneyland."

Again, Veronica made that funny choking noise, but the girls didn't stop to listen. A limo was waiting to drive them to Skye, and he needed them immediately.

"OOOOOH." STEVIE SETTLED back against the plush blue upholstery of the limo. "This is getting to feel just like home."

"Don't get too comfortable, Stevie, or it'll be tough readjusting to your usual place on the backseat of your mom's station wagon," Carole said with a laugh.

"I know," agreed Stevie. "But I can enjoy it while it lasts! All this luxury and no Veronica!"

"She looked pretty green, didn't she?" Carole giggled.

"For once she was envious of something we were doing instead of trying to make us jealous of her," Lisa replied. "I loved every minute of it!"

They settled back and looked through the tinted windows as Stephan drove smoothly along the highway. People turned and stared at the limo as it passed, curious to get a glimpse of the passengers inside.

Stevie chuckled. "Look! I bet everybody thinks we're somebody famous."

"Well, we are famous in our own way," said Carole. "We're very famous to three horses that are traveling somewhere between here and Virginia."

"That's right," said Lisa. "We're big stars to those guys!"

After a few minutes Stephan pulled off the highway and down a long road with huge empty parking lots on either side.

Again, Lisa leaned forward out of the overstuffed sofa. "Is this Ashford Racetrack, Stephan?"

"Yes, it is. Racing season won't start for another month or two, so it looks deserted." Stephan pointed to one corner of the parking lot, where a number of trailers and sound trucks were parked. "Right now, though, it's the perfect place to make a movie."

Stephan steered the big car close to the trailers. Just as he was about to turn off the engine, a young man dressed in shorts and a Skye Ransom T-shirt came running up.

"Hi, Stephan," he said, grinning at the older man. "Is this Skye's precious cargo?"

"It is." Stephan turned off the engine and got out of the car to open the girls' door. "May I present Misses Lisa, Carole, and Stevie, The Saddle Club."

"Hi, girls. I'm Jess Morton, Skye's assistant. Welcome to our set." Grinning, he shoved a clipboard under one arm and stuck out his hand.

"Hi," the girls said, shaking hands.

"Skye's sorry he couldn't meet you himself, but he's shooting a scene right now. He sent me over to get you acquainted with everything."

"Will he be shooting for a long time?" asked Lisa.

Jess shrugged wearily. "On this set, you never can tell. How about I give you the ten-cent tour until he can join us?"

The girls smiled. "Sure," Lisa said. "That sounds wonderful."

"Well, we have to walk by today's location before we can get to the stable, so why don't we start there?"

"Great," said Stevie and Carole together.

They said good-bye to Stephan and followed Jess over to a roped-off area of the parking lot. Though The Saddle Club had been on movie sets before, this one seemed bigger than any they'd ever seen. All sorts of people hurried past them, each with different jobs to do. Assistants clutching newly typed script pages ran by, while set carpenters carried long planks of lumber and plywood. Jess pointed out the boom mikes that hung overhead and the thick electrical cables coiled along the ground like giant tree roots. He walked The Saddle Club through several different interior sets, all the while dodging makeup people and sound engineers and several assistant directors.

"Gosh," said Stevie, hungrily eyeing a row of food vans that lined one end of the parking lot. "This is like a mini city all by itself."

"You're absolutely right," said Jess. "And we're not really even on location. Sometimes, when you're filming far from the studio, the set really does become your own private city."

He opened a gate and led them through some tall green hedges. "Here's a part you'll really enjoy."

They followed Jess through the hedges to a large grandstand, through a short tunnel beneath the stadium, and then they were standing just behind the starting gate of Ashford Racetrack.

"Here it is," he said with a grin. "The famous Ashford mile and a quarter. Lots of terrific racehorses have run here."

"I know," said Carole. "Whirlaway and Seabiscuit and Man O'War and Ruffian."

The girls watched as two riders wearing the orange work jackets of the Ashford track exercised their horses in an easy canter around the wide track.

"This is beautiful," said Stevie. "It makes me miss Belle. I wonder where she is."

"She's probably in Oklahoma now," Carole assured her, "just watching the oil wells pass by."

Jess smiled. "Is Belle your horse?" When Stevie nodded, he asked, "Well, do you want to see the stables? There are lots of horses over there. Skye told me that that would be the tour highlight for you."

"He knows us well," Carole replied eagerly.

They followed Jess across the racetrack and around a huge paddock to an old, elegant stable. The walls were solid mahogany, and all the door hinges were brightly polished brass. Big buckets of golden yellow chrysanthemums stood by each horse's stall, and the sounds of Mozart floated through the air.

"Hey, sounds like Ashford track stole your idea." Stevie nudged Carole gently.

Jess frowned. "What idea?"

Carole gave a sheepish grin. "It's a new theory I read about," she explained. "If you listen to certain pieces of Mozart, you'll calm down. Other pieces are supposed to raise your IQ. I figure if it works for people, then it might work for horses, too."

Stevie grinned. "So what did you tape for our guys? The smart pieces or the relaxing pieces?"

"Actually, I taped both," said Carole.

"Wonderful." Lisa laughed. "We should have three calm, brilliant horses by Thursday. I can't wait to see what they'll be like."

"I just can't wait to see them, period," grumbled Stevie.

They walked down the aisle of the stable, introducing themselves to the horses. All were magnificent Thoroughbreds with long, slender legs bred for the track. The first one, a red bay stallion named Kublai Khan, stamped his foot when they looked in his stall. Next to him, a calmer gray gelding named Silverado munched on some hay.

"Hey, look at this one," Lisa said, pausing at the stall next to Silverado. "She reminds me of Prancer."

The girls stopped and peered in the stall. Inside, a white-faced bay mare stood watching them, her tail twitching, her ears flicking in several different directions.

"She looks a little like Prancer," admitted Carole. "But she sure doesn't act much like Prancer."

"That's Mabel," Jess explained. "She's one of the stars of the movie."

"Mabel?" Stevie wrinkled her nose. "That's a pretty frumpy name for a Thoroughbred."

"You know names don't matter, Stevie," Carole reminded her, trying to pat Mabel's nose. "Neither does color. What matters with horses is heart and character."

"And whether or not they like Mozart," Lisa added with a laugh.

Someone coughed right behind them. Everyone turned. A tall man in a black sweater and tan breeches stood there frowning at them.

"Hi, George," Jess said. "These are Skye's guests

from Virginia. Girls, this is George Gamble, the stable manager for the set."

"Hi, Mr. Gamble." Carole smiled. "You've got some great-looking horses here."

"You sure do," Stevie chimed in. "It must be wonderful to work with both horses and movies."

"Does Skye get to ride all these horses?" Lisa asked.

"Not a chance." Mr. Gamble looked at them coldly, smoothing his small black mustache.

"Which ones does he ride?" asked Carole. "And what kind of schedule do you put movie horses on? When do they exercise?"

Mr. Gamble ignored her questions and glanced at his watch.

"What about Mabel?" Stevie persisted, noticing that the mare had grown more agitated when Mr. Gamble had appeared. "She seems pretty high-strung for the movies."

"Mabel has her own training schedule," Mr. Gamble muttered, again glancing at his watch. He turned to Jess. "These horses are due to be fed and groomed in about five minutes. They've got early calls tomorrow. Why don't you give Skye's little friends a barn tour some other time?"

"Sure, George," Jess said. "I didn't think—"

"No, of course you didn't." Mr. Gamble turned to the girls. "If you'll excuse us . . . Just follow Jess

34

here out of the stable area." He pointed his riding crop back toward the racetrack and then strode off in the direction of the feed room.

"Gosh," said Stevie, "I guess he didn't want his stars disturbed." She watched closely as Mr. Gamble opened the feed room door, then slammed it shut. "You know, there's something familiar about him."

"You're probably thinking of his brother," Jess said.

Stevie was about to ask who his brother was when a familiar voice rang out behind them.

"Hey, girls!"

They turned to see Skye, grinning his famous million-dollar smile and holding three delicate pink roses. "A rose for each of you," he said. "Thanks a million for coming!"

"Oh, Skye, it's so great to see you!" Lisa ran forward and gave him a hug, then Carole and Stevie did the same. Soon they were all holding each other, glad to be together again.

"Did you have trouble finding us?" asked Carole, holding the rose Skye had given her.

He shook his curly blond head and laughed. "Not a bit. After my scene was over I just headed straight for the barn." He glanced at the horses. "I knew you would want to meet the real stars of the show."

"Well, they are important cast members," said Stevie, laughing.

"Yeah," said Carole. "We got a real kick out of meeting Mabel."

"I've gotten my own kicks from meeting Mabel," agreed Skye. "Mostly from Mabel herself."

"Really?" Carole asked. "I wouldn't think they would want vicious horses on a set."

Skye frowned with concern. "I don't think she's really mean. In her stall or the paddock, she's jumpy, but okay. When you ride her out on the track with other horses, though, watch out! She spooks like crazy."

"Do you have a lot of scenes with her?" asked Lisa.

Skye nodded sadly. "That's the worst part. She's the horse I have to ride in this movie. I'm supposed to be training her for a big race. But with other horses around, I can barely get her to stand still, much less gallop around a track."

"Sounds like you need our help," said Stevie, frowning at Mabel.

"Do you really think you could come up with something?" For the first time, a gleam of hope appeared in Skye's gorgeous blue eyes.

"I've never known us not to." Stevie grinned. "And three heads are at least twice as good as one."

"Huh?" Lisa and Carole frowned.

"Oh, you know what I mean," giggled Stevie. "Just give us a little time to think about this, Skye."

"That would be wonderful." Skye smiled, but he still looked around the stable nervously. "Why don't we talk about it someplace private—like over dinner tonight?"

Stevie frowned. "But why can't we—"

"That would be great, Skye," Lisa said quickly, shooting a glance at Stevie. "We'd really enjoy that."

"Super." Skye gave a big sigh of relief. "Now that we've got that settled, why don't we walk back over to the set, and I'll introduce you to some of my friends."

Stevie frowned once at Carole, but they fell into step behind Lisa and Skye. Soon they were out of the sweet-smelling barn and back dodging cables and mikes on the movie set.

"Hey, Sherry," Skye called to a beautiful redheaded girl who was reading a script in a folding chair. "I'd like you to meet some friends of mine from Virginia." Skye put his arms around the girls. "Stevie, Carole, and Lisa, this is Sherry Lissom. She plays my girl-friend in the movie."

"Hi." Sherry gave them all a warm smile. "Welcome to our crazy set. Has Skye introduced you to everybody?"

"Well, we've met the horses," Stevie replied.

"Oh, they're Skye's favorites," Sherry giggled. "I kind of prefer the two-legged members of the cast."

37

"I guess not everybody can be a horseperson," said Carole.

"Not everybody can ride as well as Skye, either," added Sherry with a grin. She was just about to say something else when a short girl wearing a headset tapped Skye on the shoulder.

"Hey, Skye, Shev's looking for you."

"Oh, thanks, Jean." Skye grinned at the girl. "Let me introduce my friends from Willow Creek, Virginia."

"Hi!" The short girl grinned and shook hands with each of them. "Nice to meet you. I'm Jean Williams, a production assistant. Could you please make sure Skye gets over there to that bald-headed guy with the megaphone?"

"Sure," said Lisa, peering over to where Jean pointed.

"He's the assistant director," Jean explained as she hurried away. "He needs to see Skye ASAP."

Skye shrugged. "Well, let's go. You can meet Shev Bayliss, one of our directors."

They picked their way across a set that looked like a jockey's locker room. Shev Bayliss was sitting with his back to them and was having an intense conversation with a woman with short black hair.

Skye coughed. "Shev?" he asked softly. "You wanted to see me?"

Shev jumped as if he'd been caught with his hand in the cookie jar. The girls noticed a blush on the woman's pale cheeks.

"What?" Shev turned around, angry at being interrupted. When he saw Skye, his eyes grew even darker. "Oh, Ransom. It's you."

"Jean said you were looking for me?"

Shev started to speak; then he noticed Lisa, Stevie, and Carole, all standing behind Skye. "Who are these people?" he asked coldly.

"These are some friends from Virginia," Skye said. "Girls, this is Shev Bayliss, our assistant director, and Marcella DuBois, the animal coordinator."

"Hi," the girls said politely.

Marcella nodded and adjusted her short skirt. Shev just looked at them.

"They're not going to be problems on the set, are they?" he asked Skye. "You've got a rehearsal in about five minutes."

"No, Shev," Skye replied. "They'll be leaving in just a little while."

"Good." Shev glanced once more at the girls. "I'll talk to you after your friends leave," he said, turning back to Marcella with a dismissive gesture.

"Come on," said Skye. He put his arms around all three girls and led them back out to where Stephan was waiting by the car. "Sorry about that," he said as

39

they threaded their way among the cables. "Some of the people on this set are great. Others remind me of a certain part of a horse's anatomy."

"Wow, Skye," said Lisa, shocked. "Those people act so hateful toward you. I thought movie sets were supposed to be lots of fun."

"They can be," Skye replied, then looked over his shoulder. "It just all depends on who you're working with." He turned back to the girls and grinned. "Anyway, we can talk more about this at dinner tonight. I've already had Jess arrange with Stephan to drop you at the restaurant at eight."

"Uh, there's just one teeny-tiny problem with that, Skye," Lisa said, exchanging an embarrassed glance with Carole and Stevie.

"Oh no!" cried Skye. "Don't tell me you've got other plans."

"It's nothing like that," Lisa replied quickly. "It's just that there's one other person with us. I know Max and Deborah are planning to have dinner with some of their Pony Club friends. If we eat with you, then that will leave this other person all by herself."

"Oh, that's not a problem." Skye grinned. "Just bring her along, too."

"We'll bring her along, but please don't hold us responsible for her behavior," said Stevie. "This is the worst, most spoiled girl at Pine Hollow. Maybe even the whole world."

"Ah, my friend Veronica! It'll be fun to cross swords with her again. Besides, she can't be any worse than some of the people around here." Skye gave them all another quick hug and said, "I've got to go now, but I'll see *all* of you at eight o'clock sharp."

"WHAT DO YOU recommend tonight, Jacques?" Skye looked up from the thick menu at the waiter who was hovering over the table.

"Well, Monsieur Ransom, your favorite, the chicken *à l'orange*, is quite good. We also have some fresh mountain trout and some lamb chops *aux fines herbes*."

"Hmmm," said Skye as the tall candles on the elegantly set table flickered. He looked over at the girls. "What is The Saddle Club having tonight?"

"Everything sounds delicious," said Lisa. "But I think I'll have the trout."

"Me too," Carole added.

"I'd like the chicken *à l'orange*," said Stevie, wondering why the waiter was just nodding and not scribbling on a notepad.

"That sounds good to me, too." Skye turned toward the fifth person at the table. "Veronica?"

"I'd like the *ragoût fin, s'il vous plaît*," Veronica ordered in her best French accent. *"Avec des pommes vapeur et une salade panachée."*

*"Oui, mademoiselle."* The waiter clicked his heels together and disappeared as another server put two large baskets of warm French bread on their table.

Stevie frowned. "What did you order, Veronica? I couldn't tell anything about it."

Veronica rolled her eyes at Skye as she answered Stevie sarcastically. "It's a pretty elementary French dish, Stevie. You would know it if you'd paid more attention in Ms. Lebrun's class."

Stevie opened her mouth to respond, but she felt Lisa's toe poking her leg under the table.

"Tell us all about your movie, Skye," Lisa said. "The sets and horses looked fascinating, but we couldn't tell much about the plot."

Skye took a big drink of water and sighed. "Well, if I could just figure out what I'm doing wrong, it could be really great. The character I play, C.G., is a hopeful trainer and jockey. C.G.'s father was a trainer as well, but he was accused of shady dealings in the race world and killed himself because of it."

"Oh no." Carole frowned. "How awful."

"I know. Anyway, C.G. loves the horse business as much as his father did, and he wants to do great things, but he's got to live down his father's legacy. He's at the starting gate of his career, with one chance to succeed and establish his own reputation. If he can ride this one horse and win, he'll be well on his way."

Stevie interrupted. "And this horse is played by the infamous Mabel?"

"Right." Skye sighed. "This race means everything, but two other trainers at the track are doing everything they can to see that C.G. fails. Turns out that these two trainers were the ones who fudged the business when his father was accused, and they're afraid C.G. will find out the truth." Skye stared at the bread basket, his expression suddenly serious. "Their best chance is to make me fail and drive me out of the business as well."

"What happens next?" asked Carole.

"Well, while I keep Mabel's true ability a secret from them, I manage to fall in love with one of their daughters, played by Sherry." He laughed. "It's kind of a Romeo and Juliet thing."

"And?" Stevie hunched forward on the edge of her seat.

"And just before I ride Mabel to an amazing victory in the race, I learn the critical piece of evidence that clears my father's name and will ultimately convict the bad guys."

"So you ride off into the sunset with the girl and the horse and the trophy," Carole guessed.

"Right." Skye grinned. "It's a pretty well-written script, and it should do well at the box office." He sighed and shook his head. "It's too bad the set is so odd. Half the crew act like they hate me."

"I can't believe anybody could hate you, Skye!" Lisa glanced at her friends. They were finally about to get to the mystery of all this.

Skye broke off a piece of bread. "Well, they do. There's this guy on the set, George Gamble. He's the trainer for all the horses in the movie."

"We met him," said Stevie. "I could have sworn I recognized him from somewhere else."

Skye smiled. "Well, the reason you think that is—"

"Really, Stevie, how could you possibly think you know a horse trainer for the movies?" Veronica interrupted with a snide little laugh. "I mean, you've barely been out of Virginia."

Skye frowned at Veronica, then turned back to Stevie. "Anyway, George has acted like he's resented me from the first day of filming. And now Shev and Marcella are acting weird, too."

"Weird like how?" asked Carole.

Skye shrugged. "I don't know. They aren't friendly at all. If a take doesn't go well, they always blame me.

45

Yesterday a couple of horses messed up a scene that I wasn't even in, and they told everybody it was my fault!"

Lisa reached over and gave Skye's hand a supportive squeeze. "I bet they're just jealous," she said. "You've got more talent in your little finger than they do in their whole bodies, and they're just envious!"

"She's right, Skye," agreed Carole. "After all, isn't moviemaking a pretty cutthroat business?"

Skye laughed. "You've got that right. I guess this is just the first time my throat's been the one getting cut!" He made a funny face, then a whole fleet of waiters streamed out of the kitchen, bringing their dinner to the table.

"Wow," said Lisa after five huge plates of scrumptious-looking food had been spread out before them. "This looks wonderful."

"Everything smells delicious!" Carole said as she took a bite of perfectly cooked trout.

Stevie looked over at Veronica's plate, which was covered in a strange multicolored stew. "What did you say that was again, Veronica?"

"*Ragoût fin,*" Veronica replied, lifting up one pale green morsel of food with her fork. "We often have it at home. I'm sure you're familiar with it, Skye—"

"Hey, look," said Skye as a group of people sat down at a nearby table. "There are some people from the production. Excuse me for a moment, girls."

46

They watched as Skye got up and greeted the new-comers. None of their faces looked familiar. Apparently, these were people they had not met earlier.

"I guess that's all we'll find out about Skye's set problems tonight," whispered Stevie as Skye shook hands with a heavyset gray-haired man.

"I think we've found out enough," said Lisa. "I mean, he definitely needs some Saddle Club help."

"Maybe if we can help him work out his problems with Mabel, then the other problems will go away," suggested Carole.

"Well, that's something The Saddle Club can certainly do," Stevie replied, shooting a look at Veronica. "We may not know movies, but we sure know about difficult horses."

"Then we'll have to do everything we can to help him with Mabel," said Lisa.

They returned to their meals as Skye came back to the table.

"Sorry," he said, replacing his napkin on his lap. "That was my producer. I had to go and say hello."

"I understand perfectly," cooed Veronica, daintily taking a bite of her stew. "Business always comes before pleasure. That's the way it is when you're successful. Why, if I could tell you the number of times Daddy—"

"Anyway," Skye continued. "That's the story. If I could just figure out what's wrong with Mabel, then maybe certain people on the set would stop thinking I was a jerk."

"I bet we could figure out what's bugging Mabel," Stevie said.

"You think so?" Skye grinned his famous movie-star smile. "Anything you could do would really help me out."

"Well, first we have to figure out exactly what her bad habits are," said Carole.

"Yes," Veronica chimed in. "Like when Red O'Malley figured out that Danny didn't like to pull on the right side of a cart."

"What does Mabel like to eat?" asked Stevie. "I broke one of Belle's bad habits by treating her with bits of carrot."

"So far her favorite snack has been me." Skye laughed and held up one nipped finger.

"Well, we'll have to break her of that," said Carole. "But that's easy. What else does she do?"

Skye sighed. "She kicks and bites around other horses, she can't stand to have her ears touched, and once you dismount, she tries to run away."

"Whoa," said Carole. "Sounds like you might need a horse whisperer."

"A what?" Skye frowned.

"A horse whisperer," repeated Carole. "Haven't you ever heard of Monty Roberts's famous join-up method?"

Skye shook his head. The girls looked at each other, then suddenly everyone was talking at once.

"If she wants to kick, you've got to keep her moving forward," said Carole, spooning sour cream onto her baked potato.

"Or turn her in a big circle," added Lisa. She took a bite of her fish. "Keep her too busy to get into any mischief."

"Remember when Belle got that big crush on Starlight and she wouldn't leave his side for weeks?" Stevie laughed as she buttered a piece of bread.

"Red told me that if your horse tries to bite the horse in front of you, then you need to close your legs around him and keep close contact with his mouth." Veronica tried to sound as if she knew as much about horses as the other girls did. Nobody paid any attention to her.

The rest of the evening flew by. The girls told Skye all about their problems with Belle, Starlight, Danny, and Prancer and how they'd managed to solve them. By the time the waiter came to gather their plates, Skye looked like his old self again, smiling, laughing, and happy.

"Was everything to your satisfaction?" the waiter asked as he began to remove their plates.

"Everything was wonderful," said Skye.

"Oh, yes," agreed Lisa. "I've never had a more delicious meal."

"I have one question," said Stevie, looking at Veronica's empty plate.

"*Oui, mademoiselle?*" The waiter's dark eyes flashed.

"I'd like to know what was in her dish of *ragoût fin.*"

"Oh, it is wonderful." The waiter beamed. "It is full of the freshest asparagus and mushrooms and butter and sweetbreads."

Stevie frowned. "Sweetbreads?"

"*Oui, mademoiselle.* Sweetbreads."

Stevie looked at Veronica, who looked as puzzled as she did. "I'm sorry, but I'm not sure what sweetbreads are."

"Uh, they are glands, *mademoiselle.*"

"Glands?" Stevie looked in horror at Veronica's plate.

"*Oui.* The thymus gland of a calf." The waiter kissed his fingertips. "*Magnifique,* if I do say so myself."

"*Magnifique,* indeed," chuckled Stevie as Veronica turned another intense shade of green. "I know my friend enjoyed them very much."

5

"Max?" Stevie tapped softly on Max's door. "Are you awake?"

She pressed her ear against the door. For a moment she heard nothing, then she heard the sound of a lock being turned.

"What's the matter?" The door cracked open. "Is something wrong?" Max poked his head out into the hallway. His eyes were heavy with sleep, and he'd slung a blue bathrobe around him.

"No, Max, everything's fine," Stevie whispered. "We just wondered if you would take us to the Ashford track."

"The Ashford track?" Max frowned at his wrist, but he wasn't wearing his watch. "What time is it?"

"It's a little past five A.M. We wanted to get there early to help Skye with his horse, Mabel."

Max rubbed his eyes as if this were some kind of bad dream. "Aren't you guys riding in the Pony Club mounted games at eleven? I've got some horses lined up for you."

"Yes, we're looking forward to it. But we need to help Skye out first. If we could get a couple of hours in before the Pony Club games, it would be perfect." Stevie smiled up at him. "Please? It's just me and Carole and Lisa. Veronica's sleeping in."

Max shook his head and yawned. "Oh, okay. I'm up anyway. Meet me downstairs at the rental car in ten minutes."

"Thanks, Max," Stevie said as she hurried back to her room. "You're terrific!"

By five-thirty Max had dropped them at the track and Skye was leading them toward Mabel's stall. Except for an occasional swish of a tail and chomp of hay, the group's footsteps were the only noises that echoed through the stable.

"Are we the only ones here?" whispered Carole.

"I think so," Skye whispered back. "They reserved this barn for the movie horses. All the racetrack trainers are in another barn."

"So creepy old George isn't here?" Stevie asked hopefully.

Skye shrugged. "Doesn't seem to be." He gave a

small laugh. "I've noticed George doesn't make many of the early calls."

They turned the corner and neared Mabel's stall. Already her pretty head was sticking out above the door, an anxious, worried look in her eyes.

"Uh-oh," said Skye. "I think we interrupted her beauty sleep."

"Let's all stay back here and approach her one at a time," suggested Carole. "Maybe crowds are what freak her out."

"Okay." Lisa eyed the cranky-looking horse. "Who wants to approach her first?"

"I vote for Carole," Skye said with a laugh.

Everyone turned and looked expectantly at Carole. She smiled and pulled something from the pocket of her breeches. It was a sandwich bag filled with bits of apple and carrot and several lumps of sugar.

"I figured you guys might volunteer me for this, so I came prepared. Let's see what works with Miss Mabel." She took out a small piece of carrot and slowly approached the stall, holding both hands in loose fists and not looking Mabel in the eye. The big mare stomped but didn't try to kick or shy back in her stall.

"Why is she walking like that?" whispered Skye.

"It's the Monty Roberts way," replied Stevie. "If you avoid eye contact, the horse won't feel threatened."

Slowly, Carole walked up to the stall, keeping her

gaze on the ground. Mabel watched her with her ears pricked. When Carole got to within a foot of the horse's door, she extended her outstretched palm with the carrot. Mabel made a quick lunge at the tiny morsel of food, nipping Carole's hand in the process.

"Ouch!" said Carole, jerking her hand back in spite of herself. "She certainly has a hearty appetite."

"Particularly when fingers are on the menu," chuckled Skye.

"Let's try something else," Carole said, frowning thoughtfully as Mabel chomped her carrot.

This time Carole held out a small piece of apple. Mabel again watched her like a hawk, but when she lunged for the food, Carole jerked her hand back.

"No, no, Mabel," Carole corrected softly. "That's not the way to take an apple from someone's hand."

She extended her hand again. Again Mabel watched for an opportunity to snap, and again Carole pulled her hand back. After several more tries, it occurred to Mabel that if she approached the apple slowly, it would stay in place for her to nibble.

"There." Carole smiled as the horse finally took the apple gently, with her lips barely touching Carole's hand. "Mabel's just passed her first lesson in table manners."

Grinning with delight, Skye, Stevie, and Lisa began to clap softly.

"You're really terrific, Carole," Skye said. "I didn't think I'd ever see Mabel behaving this nicely."

"Well, I don't think she's a perfect horse yet," said Carole, aware of the still-contrary gleam in Mabel's eyes. "But at least we know she's smart enough to make some progress."

For the next hour, they all worked hard with Mabel, cajoling her with bits of apple and lumps of sugar. By seven-fifteen, she allowed Skye to clip a lead line on her halter for the first time since filming had begun.

"Ta-da!" crowed Skye, excited by his success as Mabel allowed him to lead her from her stall. "It's Mabel the Wonder Horse!"

"I wouldn't go that far," laughed Carole. "Even the greenest foals permit lead lines on their halters at six months old. At this rate, I figure Mabel's only five or six years behind schedule!"

As they worked with her, Mabel became even more gentle. With lots of praise and little bits of apple, they taught her to accept Skye's leading her and brushing her long, luxurious tail. Skye had just begun to touch one of her sensitive ears when a harsh voice rang out in the stable.

"What do you think you're doing to that animal?"

They all jumped. Mabel flinched, ready to rear at a moment's notice. Skye turned around. George Gamble stood there, his mouth pulled down in an ugly frown.

"Uh, hi, George." Skye tried his best to calm Mabel and talk to George at the same time. He gave him a friendly smile. "The girls and I were just trying to get in a little extra work with Mabel. You know, gentle her a little bit."

"Oh, really?" George looked at Lisa, Carole, and Stevie and frowned even harder. "Are these girls professional trainers?"

"No—" Skye began.

"Are they accustomed to working with valuable equine actors?"

"Well, no." Again Skye tried to explain.

"Then they really don't have any business being on this set at all, do they?" George's face grew red. "And they certainly don't have any business being in a production stable at seven-thirty in the morning."

"They are my guests, George," Skye said reasonably. "They are here at my invitation."

"And they are leaving at *my* invitation!" said George, tapping his riding crop against the side of his boot.

"I think you're being unfair, George," protested Skye. "These girls are expert horsewomen. Far better riders than I am."

"It wouldn't take much to be a better rider than you, Ransom." George's upper lip curled in a snarl.

"And let me remind you that as long as I'm in charge of the horses in this production, what I say goes, as far as this stable is concerned! And they go." He glared at the girls.

For an instant, Skye's fists clenched in anger; then he turned away from George and smiled at the girls.

"I'm sorry you had to see the ugly side of filmmaking," he apologized loudly. "Let's go back to my trailer. The atmosphere is a lot friendlier there!"

With that, Skye handed Mabel's lead rope to George and led the girls back to his trailer.

"Wow," Lisa whispered as soon as they were out of George's earshot. "What's with that guy? He acts like he hates everybody!"

"Oh, I think mostly he just hates me," Skye said, shaking his head. "But apparently he can drum up a good case against my friends as well."

"Don't worry about it, Skye." Stevie gave him a reassuring smile. "He's just a jealous jerk."

"Yeah," agreed Carole. "I can tell by the way Mabel responded that you're a much better horseman than he is, any day."

When they reached Skye's trailer, they found Jess there waiting for them.

"Hey, buddy, I've got some good news for you!" he said cheerily.

"What is it?" asked Skye. "I could stand some good news right now."

Jess held up his clipboard. "This is today's shooting schedule. Guess who's name isn't on it until late this afternoon?"

"Mine?" Skye guessed, a grin spreading across his face.

"You got it, buddy. You're a free man until about four o'clock."

"Oh, Skye!" cried Lisa. "That's terrific. Why don't you come to the Pony Club rally with us?"

"That would be great," agreed Stevie. "You can cheer us on in our games!"

Skye sat down on the steps of his trailer, frowning. "That sounds like a lot of fun, but I don't know. Sometimes my appearance can be . . . I don't know . . . distracting."

Carole laughed. "You mean when thousands of female fans mob your car and scream for your autograph?"

Skye shrugged. "Well, yeah," he replied, a sheepish smile on his face. "I'd love to come, but I'd hate to mess stuff up for you guys."

"No!" Stevie cried. "That wouldn't mess anything up for us at all. In fact, any diversion you could create would definitely be to our advantage!"

Skye frowned. "How do you figure that?"

"It's easy," Lisa laughed. "If all the other girls in the mounted games can't keep their eyes off you, then our Horse Wise team is sure to win!"

Laughing, Skye shook his head. "I guess I hadn't thought of it that way, but I'll be happy to do anything that'll help your cause."

Jess laughed along with everybody else. "You want to go over to wardrobe and see if you can find something to make you look a little less like a movie star?"

"No, no!" cried Stevie. "We want him to look like a movie star!"

"I don't know." Skye shook his head. "Being mobbed by hundreds of screaming girls can be pretty scary." He looked at them. "Why don't you guys hang out in here and I'll go see what I can come up with."

"Oh, okay," said Lisa, laughing.

"If you insist," Carole agreed.

They sat down in Skye's trailer while Jess and Skye picked their way between the various surrounding trailers. Stevie sat at Skye's makeup table, staring at her reflection in the brightly lit mirror.

"Maybe I should become a movie star," she said dramatically, turning her face to one side and posing with a faraway look in her eyes. "Then thousands of screaming boys would mob me. Phil would be jealous of them all!"

"Thousands of screaming boys might be nice," agreed Lisa. "But I'm learning that there are a lot of other things about being a movie star that aren't so hot."

"Like having to put up with awful people like

59

George," said Carole, shuddering. "He was about the rudest man I've ever met."

"I know," said Stevie. "We've met some pretty strange horsepeople, but I think he's the strangest."

"He's certainly the most unfriendly," agreed Lisa.

There was a knock on Skye's trailer door. For an instant the girls looked at each other, not knowing if they should answer it or not.

"Think we should get it?" asked Lisa. "It might be George."

"I think we should." Carole nodded at Stevie, who sat closest to the door. "I mean, it might be some sort of important message for Skye."

"Okay." Stevie hopped up and pulled the door open.

Outside, a dark-haired guy wearing thick glasses grinned at her, a pizza box on his arm.

"Large anchovy and mushroom," he announced in a weird, squeaky voice.

"We didn't order any pizza," said Stevie, frowning. "It's only eight o'clock in the morning, anyway. Nobody eats pizza now."

"Well, that's what this ticket says." The young man fumbled with a slip of paper and almost dumped the pizza out on the ground. "Large anchovy and mushroom."

Lisa and Carole came over and stood behind Stevie. "Who ordered the pizza?" asked Carole.

"Uh, I don't know." The delivery guy squinted at his ticket. "It's hard to read this writing."

Lisa frowned. "You're not really a pizza delivery guy, are you? You're just somebody who thought this would be a good way to meet Skye Ransom!"

The delivery guy frowned. "Skye Ransom? Who's he?"

"Why, he's just about the most famous movie star in the world," Stevie said, her hands on her hips.

"And here he is, at your service!" The pizza delivery guy took off his glasses and fake teeth. Though his blond hair was covered with a dark wig, the girls could see Skye's sparkling blue eyes and gorgeous smile.

"Skye!" Stevie cried. "It's you!"

"Makeup did a pretty good job on short notice, didn't they?" Skye laughed as he threw the empty pizza box on the floor. "I really had you guys fooled!"

"You think you can fool a hundred sharp-eyed Pony Clubbers?" Lisa asked.

"I think I can try," Skye said. "Come on. Stephan's waiting for us in the parking lot. He's got strict orders to let us out a block from the gate so that none of the Pony Club competition will remotely suspect that they've got an actor masquerading as a fan!"

61

6

STEPHAN DROPPED Skye and The Saddle Club off a short distance from the front gate of Ashford Farms, where the Pony Club games were being held. Skye still wore his pizza delivery shirt over his riding breeches, so the stares they got from the other riders were more curious than excited. When they walked into the arena, the girls immediately began searching for Max.

"Wonder where he could be?" asked Stevie, shading her eyes against the bright sunlight.

"I don't know," said Lisa. "He should be here with Veronica and our riding helmets."

"Hi, girls," said a voice behind them. "Hi, Skye."

They turned. Max stood there, a bag of riding helmets in his hand, chuckling at Skye's dark wig and fake teeth.

62

"How did you recognize him?" cried Stevie. "We thought he was a pizza guy."

"My ESP," Max said, laughing. "After dealing with you guys, I'm ready to expect anything. Seeing Skye Ransom dressed up like a pizza dude doesn't surprise me in the least." He looked around. "Where's Veronica? You four need to hurry and get ready for these games."

Lisa looked mystified. "We thought she was coming with you, Max. She wanted to sleep in this morning."

"I knocked on her door and got no answer." Max frowned. "Maybe she's running late and is going to grab a cab over here. Carole, why don't you go give her a call? You'll have to use the pay phone; I forgot to charge my cell phone."

"Okay." Carole hurried over to a pay phone by the concession stand and dug two quarters out of her pocket. Soon the operator had connected her with their hotel, and the switchboard was ringing Veronica's room. The phone rang several times. Just as Carole began to get really worried that something serious had happened, a muffled voice croaked, "Hello?"

"Veronica?" Carole frowned. The other girl sounded weak and breathless.

"Hnnhh," Veronica groaned.

"Why are you at the hotel? You're supposed to be here at the Pony Club games. We're scheduled to compete in less than an hour."

"I'm sick." Veronica wheezed dramatically over the phone. "I was sick all night."

"Sick?" Carole pressed the phone against her ear. "But you were all right at dinner last night."

"Well, I'm sick now," moaned Veronica.

Carole felt concerned until she remembered that Veronica had looked fine before she'd found out that her *ragoût fin* had really been the thymus gland of a calf. After that, she'd turned a weird shade of green and hadn't said a word.

"Well, do you think you'll be able to ride at all today?" Carole asked. If Veronica couldn't ride, they wouldn't have the required number of riders, and Horse Wise would have to forfeit the match.

"Ride?" Veronica groaned weakly. "No. I may never ride again."

"But—" Carole began.

Veronica mumbled something about the water in California and her delicate constitution, then the phone went dead.

*Oh, no,* Carole thought. *We've got to do something, and fast!* She hung up the phone and ran back to her friends. Stevie and Lisa were talking to Skye, but Max was nowhere in sight.

"So where's Veronica?" Stevie asked, laughing at Skye's imitation of George Gamble.

"She's sick," announced Carole.

"Sick?" Lisa tucked her short blond hair behind her ears. "She was her usual rotten self last night."

"I think she's suffering from a severe case of sweet-bread surprise," Carole said. "Which would be funny, except she says she's too sick to ride."

"Oh no," groaned Stevie. "That means we'll have to forfeit."

"Unless we can find a fourth rider," said Carole.

"Who could we get?" Lisa looked around. All the other riders seemed to be with their teams, their numbers pinned to their backs. "We don't know anybody here except Max."

"How about Max?" suggested Stevie. "He's a great rider."

"Yeah, and about twenty years over the age limit," Carole replied.

"But maybe we could get Skye to make him up like a teenager," Stevie pressed on, her eyes bright.

They all looked at Skye. He had his hands on his hips, just listening to the conversation.

"Well, Skye?" Stevie asked. "What do you think?"

"I think that's the craziest idea I've ever heard," Skye replied.

"Then you come up with a better one!" cried Stevie. "You're not being very sympathetic."

"That's right, Skye," agreed Lisa. "You're in trouble and we're helping you. Why can't you help us?"

65

"Actually, that's exactly what I had in mind," he said. "But you never asked me!"

"What?" Lisa frowned, puzzled.

Carole started to laugh. "I get it!" she said. She grinned at Skye. "*He* can ride in Veronica's place. The entry form just said four riders. We didn't have to give any names!"

"What about a helmet?" asked Lisa.

"Max brought Veronica's," said Carole. "And her head's so big her helmet would fit anybody."

"Oh, you guys are brilliant!" Stevie threw her arms around Skye and gave him a hug. "Just take out those false teeth so you won't look quite so weird. I'd hate to have you scare the horses!"

"Okay." Skye spit out the goofy-looking teeth and removed his clip-on bow tie. Except for the pizza shop logo on the pocket of his shirt, he looked like a normal rider.

"Great!" Carole beamed. "Let's go get our numbers and find the horses Max borrowed for us."

A little while later, four Horse Wise team riders were lined up behind the starting line, big red 5s pinned to the backs of their shirts.

"Do you think anybody noticed you?" Stevie whispered to Skye as she looked at the other riders waiting for the races to begin.

"I don't think so." Skye pulled Veronica's helmet down lower over his dark wig. "It looks like every-

66

body's concentrating on the races. I just hope I'm good enough to help you guys out."

"You'll do fine," Carole assured him, smiling. "Just hang in there and don't get nervous. We'll tell you what to do. You know how to pretend you know what you're doing, don't you?"

"That's why they pay me the big bucks," he said, grinning.

The first race was announced. It was a keyhole race, where riders rode down a long straight path, turned their horses in a tight circle, then galloped back to the finish line. The Horse Wise team took their place behind the starting line.

"Who wants to go first?" asked Stevie.

"I will," volunteered Carole. "That way Skye can see what I'm doing. Then, Skye, you go. Then Lisa. Then, Stevie, you can bat cleanup."

"Let's just hope this horse can clean up," Stevie laughed, giving the fat little gray she was riding an affectionate pat.

The gun went off, and so did Carole. She rode her pinto mare straight down to the circle, then reined her up hard. Turning in almost a dressage pirouette, she maintained her seat perfectly, then thundered back home.

"Got it?" Stevie asked Skye as Carole raced toward them.

"Got it!" he called as Carole slapped his hand. He

kicked his buckskin gelding into a quick gallop and they were off. He didn't ride as fast or turn his mount as tightly as Carole did, but he held on and soon slapped Lisa's hand, sending her on her way. A moment later it was Stevie's turn. As the crowd cheered and riders shouted encouragement to their friends, she flew down the track. The gray turned nimbly as a cow pony, and soon they were galloping back, crossing the finish line in a blur. A moment later, she heard the announcer on the loudspeaker.

"Congratulations to the Horse Wise team from Willow Creek, Virginia, who came in first in the keyhole race!"

Stevie rode over and high-fived Carole, Lisa, and Skye. Everyone grinned, then they concentrated on catching their breath for the next race.

"Now we're going to do something a little different," the announcer called. "We're going to use the same keyhole course, but this time we're going to ride it sidesaddle. All riders have to throw their right leg and stirrup over their horses and complete the course riding modified sidesaddle."

A buzz of excitement went through the crowd as the riders adjusted their seats and tack.

"Think you can do this?" Carole asked Skye as she threw her right leg across the front of her saddle.

"I don't know," he answered in a high, feminine voice. "I've never ridden like a girl before."

68

"Actually, I've only done it a couple of times, so it's pretty new to me, too," said Lisa as she adjusted her stirrup iron and shifted her rear end over the right side of the saddle.

"It's really not that hard," Stevie said. "The trick is not to trot. Stay at a walk or canter and you'll be fine."

When everyone was seated sideways on their horses, they went back to their places behind the starting line.

"Who wants to go first this time?" asked Carole.

"Why don't you let me," said Skye. "I'll probably have to go slower. You guys can make up for my lost time."

"Okay," the girls agreed.

They pulled their horses slightly behind Skye's and waited for the race to begin. With everyone looking at the distant end of the field, the starting gun fired. Skye and his horse leaped forward.

At first the buckskin seemed confused by the odd distribution of weight in his saddle. He started off at a canter, then pulled down into a trot. For a horrible moment the girls watched Skye bobble, out of balance in the saddle, and the other horses thunder past.

"Canter!" yelled Stevie above the crowd.

She saw Skye's elbows flap out once, then he leaned forward. The buckskin took off like a rocket, his hooves kicking up little mounds of dirt. Everyone held their breath as Skye wobbled through the turn, then the buckskin dug in and they raced toward the finish line.

"Go next, Lisa!" cried Stevie as Skye came toward them with his hand extended.

Lisa rode fast, making up some lost time for Skye, then it was Stevie's turn. She, too, edged up a little on the competition, then Carole rode the anchor lap. Even riding sidesaddle, she sat her horse like a dream, but her mare stumbled coming out of the turn. By the time they crossed the finish line, the team in the next lane had taken off their helmets in triumph.

"And that race goes to the Ingleside team from Valparaiso, Indiana," the announcer proclaimed. "We'll take a fifteen-minute break here, folks, then our next race will be the costume change."

"Well, I should be more help to you with that," laughed Skye as they dismounted to let their horses drink some water. "If there's anything I learned in the theater, it's how to change costumes fast between acts!"

Fifteen minutes later, everyone lined up again. At the far end of the field stood several boxes of clothes.

"Okay, contestants. You must ride your horse to one of the boxes at the end of the field, put on pants, shirt or jacket, and a hat, and then gallop back to the starting line and tag one of your teammates. The first team that can clothe all four riders wins."

"Who wants to go first?" asked Carole.

"Let me," said Lisa. "I'm the slowest dresser. Let Skye ride anchor this time."

"Thanks." Skye grinned. "I'm glad you have so much confidence in me."

Lisa was about to say something else when the starting gun went off. She turned her pony and galloped down to the end of the field. Stevie, Carole, and Skye watched as she pulled up next to a box, got off her horse, and dug around for some clothes. Soon she'd pulled on a pair of painter's coveralls, a baseball jacket, and a stocking cap. Leaping back on her horse, she galloped back toward them.

"Go!" she said, as she crossed the starting line and slapped Stevie's hand.

Stevie raced down to the box. She returned wearing a pair of warm-up pants, a baggy sweater, and a football helmet crammed on top of her riding hat. Next it was Carole's turn. She galloped down the field, aware that the team from South Carolina was riding with them neck and neck. Quickly, she dug an old pleated skirt, frilly blouse, and woolly hat out of the clothes box, donned them, and jumped back on her horse. By the time she slapped Skye's hand, the last rider from South Carolina was halfway to the box.

"Hurry!" she cried. "They're about to beat us."

Skye squeezed his horse into a gallop, arriving at

the clothes box just as the other rider was beginning to pull on a pair of pants. In a flash, he was on the ground. Almost before anyone could blink their eyes, he was back in the saddle, wearing a suit coat and pants and a silvery top hat over his riding helmet.

"Come on, Skye!" Carole and Lisa yelled. "Hurry!"

With a final nudge at his horse, he crossed the finish line half a length in front of the rider from South Carolina.

"All right!" Stevie cried, holding her arms high above her head.

"Congratulations to the Horse Wise team," said the announcer. "Those quick-change artists are in first place as we head into our final race."

"Oh boy," said Lisa, her cheeks rosy with excitement. "Just one more race to go."

"Wonder what'll be next," said Carole. "We've done just about everything."

"Our final event will be the old egg-and-spoon race," said the announcer. "Whoever has the softest hands and steadiest nerves will win this one. Riders, be ready in about five minutes."

Skye looked at the girls. "Egg and spoon?" he asked with a frown.

"You have to carry an egg in a spoon all the way down to the end of the arena and back," explained Lisa. "If you drop it or you break your egg, you're out of the race."

"Ugh," said Skye. "That sounds a lot harder than any of the others."

"It is," agreed Stevie. "Particularly for people who don't ride every day." She frowned. "I just wish there was some way we could even the playing field, to give you a fighting chance."

Suddenly she snapped her fingers. "I've got it! You guys wait right there! I'll be back in a flash!"

Skye, Carole, and Lisa watched as Stevie trotted up toward the announcer's stand. She smiled and waved at people she didn't know, stopping to chat with some and pointing over toward the far end of the track with her crop. In a few moments, she trotted back, a wide grin on her face.

"What did you do, Stevie?" Carole frowned with suspicion. "You've got that funny grin on your face."

"Nothing," Stevie replied innocently. "Just talked to some of the other contestants. Did you know there's a rumor going around?"

"No." Lisa leaned forward. "What kind of rumor?"

"Oh, that a famous movie star is here, competing in disguise." Stevie grinned. "Somebody thought they saw him, way down at the other end of the field."

Everyone looked where Stevie pointed. Sure enough, there was a small cluster of girls and a few boys gathered around some helpless boy on a black horse.

"Stevie!" cried Carole. "You didn't!"

Stevie shrugged. "Who knows how rumors get started?"

A woman came by and gave them each an egg and a spoon, then the announcer called for attention.

"Okay, riders, the last race is about to begin. Be the first team to ride four unbroken eggs down the arena and back, and you'll win. Is everybody ready?"

Actually, only half the competitors were ready. The other half was peering at the boy on the black horse at the far end of the field.

The starting gun went off. By the time everyone realized that the race was truly under way, Skye had carried his egg halfway down the track.

"Hurry!" Lisa called. "Only hurry carefully!"

Skye rounded the barrel at the end of the arena, then started home. Soon, with his egg safely in his spoon, he crossed the finish line and tagged Lisa. She cantered away, rounding the barrel with her own egg barely wobbling. She came back and tagged Carole, who never made a false move. Then it was Stevie's turn.

"*Yee-hü!*" Stevie gave a wild Western yell as she urged her pony into an easy canter. Her egg wobbled once, but she settled down deep in the saddle and carried it without another bounce. She rounded the barrel smoothly, then cantered toward the finish line, the egg hardly moving in the spoon.

"Come on, Stevie, come on!" yelled Carole and

Lisa, aware that the fourth Sunnyside rider was gaining fast.

"Coming!" said Stevie. She looked over her shoulder once, then gave her horse an extra squeeze. They bounded over the finish line, the egg still unbroken.

"We've got our winner, folks!" the announcer cried over the speaker as Stevie accepted the congratulations of her friends. "It was close, but four blue ribbons go to the Horse Wise team from Willow Creek, Virginia, our first-place winners for the day!"

"And an extra blue ribbon for Stevie Lake," whispered Skye. "Our prizewinning gossip for the day!"

"HEY, GUYS!" MAX'S voice rang out over the crowd. "Congratulations!"

The Horse Wise team turned. Max and Deborah, carrying Maxi, walked toward them, big smiles on their faces.

"I'm so proud of you!" Max leaned forward and shook Skye's hand. "Nice job of filling in at the last minute, Skye."

"Mostly I just did what the girls told me to do," Skye admitted shyly. "And hoped I could hang on!"

"You looked like a real pro out there." Deborah gave Skye a warm smile, but there was a troubled look in her eyes.

"Is everything okay, Deborah?" Stevie asked, holding out her arms for Maxi.

"I may as well tell all of you the bad news now," Deborah said as she placed Maxi in Stevie's arms. She sighed. "I'm afraid that our horses are still somewhere between here and Willow Creek. I was supposed to meet the van an hour ago at the stable, but it hasn't shown up. I've called the shipping company, but all I get is an answering machine. Mrs. Reg is calling from Virginia, too."

"Oh no," said Stevie, wincing as Maxi tugged on a lock of her honey blond hair. "I knew something like this would happen. I knew that van driver was an idiot!"

"What'll we do, Max?" Carole cried. "We're supposed to ride tomorrow, and the horses will need to rest beforehand. We can't ride if they're woozy and exhausted from a cross-country van trip."

"I don't know," Max said, frowning deeply.

"Well, don't panic yet," said Deborah. "I'm still working on it from this end, and Mrs. Reg is on the case at the other end. Between us, we're going to make sure that something gets done!" She gave Maxi a quick kiss on her forehead. "You stay here with the girls, honey. Mommy's going to go give the shipping company a piece of her mind!"

Everyone watched as Deborah hurried over to the pay phone.

"Max, you think the horses are all right, don't you?" Lisa asked as Deborah punched in her phone card number.

"Oh, the horses will be fine, Lisa," Max said with a smile. "It's the van company I'm worried about now. With my wife calling from one coast and my mother calling from the other, those poor fools don't have a chance!"

They all laughed as Max took Maxi from Stevie's arms. "You guys have done a super job this morning— I hope you're planning to have some fun this afternoon."

Stevie frowned. "Actually, we haven't given it much thought."

"Have you given any thought to what might be wrong with Veronica?" asked Max. "Deborah talked to her, and all she would say was that she felt awful, but she wouldn't see a doctor."

Stevie looked at her friends and shrugged. "Beats me, Max," she replied. "She was fine last night before she dug into that plate of sweetbreads."

"Sweetbreads?" Max wrinkled his nose and grimaced. "Well, after Deborah reaches the trucking company, I think we're going to take Maxi to Knott's Berry Farm." He smiled at the girls and Skye. "Want to join us?"

"Thanks," Skye replied. "But I've got a late-afternoon call."

"Would you like a little more help with Mabel before you start shooting?" asked Carole.

"Sure." Skye grinned. "That would be great, if you've got the time to do it."

"How about we do Knott's Berry Farm some other time, Max?" Stevie asked. "Skye really needs our help."

"Not a problem," Max replied. "Just keep us posted where you're going to be, and we'll see you later."

He lifted Maxi into her carrier as The Saddle Club followed Skye out to the parking lot. At the very back of the lot stood Stephan, patiently waiting beside the black limo.

"Everything go well, sir?" Stephan asked, holding the door open for Skye and the girls.

"Everything went great, Stephan," Skye replied happily, gesturing toward the four blue ribbons in Stevie's hand. "For a couple of hours, I was actually having fun riding a horse."

"And doing it well, I see," said Stephan, grinning at the sea of blue.

"Oh, let's hurry back to the stable," said Lisa. "Maybe if we work hard with Mabel, you can start having fun riding her."

"I don't know." Skye gave a defeated sigh. "But I'm sure willing to try."

After just a few moments, Stephan had dropped them at the entrance of the stable. The whole place was deserted, except for the movie horses, calmly munching hay in their stalls. Slowly, the group made their way down to Mabel's stall. As soon as they got to within ten feet of her door, her head poked out and she stared at them, the whites of her eyes showing nervously.

"Oh boy," said Skye. "Looks like the old Mabel is back."

"Hang on," Carole whispered. "Give her a chance to get used to us again."

The others stood back while Carole approached Mabel using the Monty Roberts way, not looking at the mare and keeping her fingers curled close to her palms. At first Mabel looked frightened; then, as Carole drew closer, her ears began to twitch forward with interest and her eyes showed less alarm.

"Good girl," Carole said softly, still not looking directly into Mabel's face. "How about some nice apple?"

She held out a tiny bit of apple on her palm. At first Mabel acted as if she were going to lunge forward and grab the snack along with a few of Carole's fingers, but suddenly she seemed to remember her previous lesson. Gently, she reached forward and took the apple, her lips barely brushing against Carole's hand.

"Good girl!" Carole reached up and rubbed Mabel's soft nose. "You remembered!"

"Wow!" said Skye, amazed at the suddenly calm and docile horse. "That's terrific!"

"Why don't you come feed her some apple, Skye?" suggested Carole. "That way you two can become friends."

Stevie and Lisa watched as Skye stepped forward and gave Mabel some apple in the same way Carole had. After a few minutes Mabel was eating out of his hand, and just a little while later she'd allowed him to clip a line to her halter and lead her out of the stall.

"Oh, Skye," Lisa whispered as he led Mabel past her, "this is so wonderful! She's like a totally different animal!"

Skye smiled, but the expression froze on his face as angry words rang out behind them.

"What in the world is going on here?"

Everyone turned. George Gamble stood there, his face red with rage.

"Who are you?" he demanded, staring straight at Skye. "And how dare you touch that horse! Do you have any idea how much that animal is worth?"

Stevie glanced at Lisa. Skye hadn't bothered to remove his wig or his pizza delivery shirt. George didn't seem to recognize him!

"Uh, I'm j-just a f-friend of theirs." Skye pretended to stutter nervously at George's rampage.

"Yes, and I know exactly who they are," George

snarled, turning toward the girls. "They are the so-called friends of the great Skye Ransom, that incompetent who thinks he can invite total strangers into my stable and meddle with my horses!"

"We were j-just petting her," Skye stuttered again, staying in his role as the pizza guy.

"Yeah, I bet you were." George stalked over and grabbed the lead rope from Skye's hands, and Mabel whinnied with fear. "If Fred were here this wouldn't happen. I wouldn't have to put up with this nonsense from people who just wander in from Virginia and poke their noses where they don't belong!"

As Stevie watched George tug Mabel back to her stall, she realized why he looked so familiar to her— the black hair, the dark, brooding eyes, the slightly crooked nose looked just like Fred Gamble's, another young actor who had played a number of roles similar to Skye's. Though the fan magazines called them rivals, Fred had never been cast in any of the good roles that Skye had gotten, and he'd never shown any particular acting talent on the screen. However, if George was Fred's brother, then he would think that Fred should have been cast in this role instead of Skye. So he was making life hard for Skye on purpose. If Skye got fired from the movie, Fred could come in and take his place! Stevie jumped as George slammed Mabel's stall door shut. This was the meanest, most underhanded plot she'd ever discovered!

"All of you have about thirty seconds to get out of here!" George growled. "And if I ever see any of you in this barn again, I'm calling the police!"

"C-Come on," Skye said shakily, still pretending to be a dork. "He means business!"

They hurried out of the stable while George watched them go. Back in the bright sunshine, Carole spotted a shady hill that overlooked the stable and racetrack. It looked just like the hill they sat on so often in Virginia.

"Come on!" she said, tugging at Skye's shirtsleeve. "Saddle Club meeting. Now!"

Without another word, they hurried to the top of the hill and sat down beneath a shady oak tree. As they caught their breath they could see George storming out of the stable and over into one of the movie trailers.

"What is going on?" Lisa cried. "That guy is the rudest person I've ever met in my life!"

"That's George Gamble," explained Skye. "You might have heard of his little brother."

"You mean Fred Gamble, the actor?" Stevie asked, her eyes bright.

Skye nodded. "My big rival in Hollywood."

"You're kidding!" Lisa cried. "That guy is Fred Gamble's brother?"

"He sure is. And remember Marcella, the girl who was flirting with Shev Bayliss?"

Stevie frowned—she hadn't realized that Shev and Marcella were an item—but Carole and Lisa nodded.

"Well, she's Fred and George's sister."

Carole lifted an eyebrow. "But if she's the film's animal coordinator, isn't she George's boss?"

Skye nodded. "That's right. They both signed on to do this movie thinking Fred would get the part. But the producer hired me instead, and they've been furious ever since."

"And that's why they're making your life miserable," said Lisa. "If you fail and get fired, then Fred can take over your role."

Skye sighed and threw a pebble down the hill. "That's about the size of it."

"Wow!" Carole slumped back against the tree. "We're up against a whole lot more than just retraining a nervous mare. We need to retrain a whole bunch of powerful people!"

For a moment they all just stared at the stable, watching as one of George's assistants led a horse out for some exercise.

"What can we do?" said Lisa. "I've never tried to reeducate grown-ups in basic stuff like manners and respect."

Stevie snapped her fingers. "I know! If our own horses ever get here from Virginia, we could have the van drivers come over here to the set. Then we could lure George and Shev and Marcella into the trailer and lock the door! Then we could tell the van driver to take them up to Anchorage, Alaska. By the time they got there, the movie would already be made!"

Everyone looked at Stevie for a moment, then they burst out laughing.

"That's a great idea, Stevie," chuckled Skye. "But this is really a horse problem more than a people problem. Pretty soon I'm going to have to ride Mabel in a race. Not only will I have to stay on, but I'm going to have to win, and win convincingly."

"But nobody else in the movie will really be trying to beat you, will they?" asked Carole.

"No," Skye admitted. "We'll all be pretending. But I will have to get Mabel to gallop without throwing me. Maybe I should just give up and get them to use a stunt double instead of trying to ride in the race myself. But I hate to do it—it feels like cheating somehow. And I *know* I can ride convincingly if I could just get the chance."

"Of course you can," Lisa said firmly. "And we were making some progress today. I mean, Mabel did let you snap a line on her and lead her out of her stall."

"Yeah, and then George stormed in and scared the poor horse half to death," said Carole. "Mabel probably doesn't know what to think, now."

"Are you sure you don't want to try my shove-everybody-in-an-In-Transit-van scheme?" Stevie asked hopefully.

"Sorry, Stevie." Skye gave a sad sigh. "As much as I would like to, I just don't think it'll work."

"Well, then." Stevie looked at Carole and Lisa. "I guess The Saddle Club will just have to put our heads together and come up with another plan."

# 8

"GOOD GRIEF, STEVIE!" Carole said, looking at the bowl of multicolored food on Stevie's breakfast plate. "That looks as strange as what Veronica ordered the other night."

"It's my own creation," replied Stevie, stirring the stuff with her spoon. "It's granola with yogurt and different kinds of jam." She took a bite and grinned. "I've got blueberry and strawberry and apricot all mixed up together."

"And it tastes okay?" Lisa asked as the waitress brought her a simple plate of scrambled eggs and bacon.

"Tastes great," Stevie mumbled, her mouth full. "I may write this recipe down and have it for breakfast every morning at home."

"Whatever." Carole looked at Lisa and shook her head.

"Morning, girls," a familiar voice called. Everyone looked up as Max pulled out the chair beside Stevie. He carried Maxi and a cell phone in his arms. "How is everybody this morning?"

"Oh, fine." Lisa smiled. "We're just watching Stevie eat. It's gotten to be one of our favorite pastimes."

Max didn't even bother to glance at Stevie's bowl. He looked at the girls and started talking.

"I'm afraid I've got some bad news. Our horses have not arrived."

"Not arrived?" cried Carole. "What do you mean?"

"Well, both Deborah and my mother have been on the phone with these jokers for the past twenty-four hours. They've learned that the horses are in good condition, but there was a rock slide on the interstate in Arkansas and some kind of huge traffic jam in Oklahoma. The horses are definitely late, but nothing has been the van company's fault."

"But won't it be their fault if Veronica doesn't get to ride this afternoon?" asked Lisa. "She can't ride if her horse isn't anywhere in sight."

"I wouldn't worry about it, since Veronica isn't anywhere in sight, either," said Stevie. "By the way, where is she?"

"She's still holed up in her room." Max shifted

Maxi to his other knee. "She finally saw the hotel doctor last night. He said she had nothing serious, just a touch of the stomach flu."

"More like a touch of sweetbreads," chuckled Stevie as she stirred her yogurt again.

"It's just too bad that we've come all the way across the country and poor Veronica can't even compete," said Lisa. Then she frowned. "Wait! It's not only Veronica today. It's Carole, too! You were signed up for the same hunter-jumper class as Veronica, weren't you?"

Carole sighed and nodded.

"And now you won't be able to compete either, because Starlight is in the middle of a traffic jam somewhere in Oklahoma."

"Well, I've been in lots of competitions," Carole said softly. "And I'll be in lots more. Missing one isn't going to kill me." She looked at the others, then she began to blink back tears. "I am beginning to worry about Starlight, though. He and the other horses have been in that trailer an awfully long time."

"Hi, everybody."

The girls looked up. Deborah stood there, her mouth curled down in a disgusted line. Max pulled out the chair beside him and motioned for her to sit down.

"I just wanted to let you guys know that I've got good news and bad news."

"Are the horses okay?" Carole blurted out as Stevie froze with her spoon halfway between her yogurt and her mouth.

Deborah gave a soft smile. "Oh, yes," she assured Carole. "The horses are fine."

"Thank heavens!" said Stevie.

"I just finished talking to the man who is actually driving the van that's carrying the horses. He said he was terribly sorry for all the delays, and he's expecting to arrive first thing in the morning."

"Did he give any explanation for why the horses aren't here now?" asked Lisa.

"He said he got poor instructions from the first driver," reported Deborah.

"I knew it!" cried Stevie. "That guy was a nitwit! He didn't even know where California was!"

"Well, he's no longer with the company," said Deborah. "The man I talked to assured me that the horses are fine and healthy. In fact, he's going to stop for the night at a place where he can let them out into a paddock so they'll have some kind of a break from the trip."

"I don't know," Carole worried out loud. "I still wish there was some way we could really find out if our horses were okay."

"I heard each of them on the guy's cell phone," said Deborah.

"Huh?" Max looked at her. "You talked to the horses?"

"I sure did," replied Deborah. "I told him I wasn't going to be satisfied until I heard each one snort, whinny, and munch. He took his cell phone to each stall, and I heard good, healthy sounds from each." She looked at the girls and laughed. "Although, to be honest, I wasn't absolutely positive I could tell the difference between Danny's snort and Belle's nicker."

The girls looked at each other, then began to laugh. Maxi was laughing right along with them when Max's cell phone chirped.

"Hold her a minute," he said, passing Maxi to Deborah as he flipped open the phone.

"Hello?" he said into the tiny receiver. "Oh, hi, Mom!"

The girls could hear the sound of Mrs. Reg's voice all the way across the table.

"You talked to the driver of the van?" Max winked as Mrs. Reg continued. "And he told you he'd be here tomorrow, and that everything was fine?"

Max nodded as his mother talked on. "And even though he thought you were crazy, you made him take his cell phone around to each stall so that you could hear each individual horse?"

The girls giggled. Mrs. Reg had done exactly the same thing Deborah had!

Grinning, Max kept repeating what Mrs. Reg was saying. "He said, 'I'll do it, but you won't be able to tell the difference between any of them!' "

Max listened a moment, than laughed. "Say that again, Mom. I want the girls to hear you."

He held the phone in the middle of the breakfast table. Mrs. Reg's voice came through loud and clear. "He didn't think I would know the difference between Danny and Belle and Prancer and Starlight! Imagine! Of course I know the difference. And all four are absolutely fine!"

"LADIES AND GENTLEMEN, our last contestant in today's final event is Alana White from San Antonio, Texas, riding her horse, Spirit." The announcer's voice rang over the arena as a small, trim rider guided her prancing black Arabian into the ring.

"Wow," Carole breathed. "What a wonderful-looking pair."

"I know," said Lisa. "They're so far ahead in points they could do this course at a walk and still win."

"I'm hot," grumbled Stevie, digging in her backpack for a bottle of water. "I'm glad this is the last event."

Lisa turned and frowned. "Haven't you enjoyed this, Stevie? I feel like I've learned tons of stuff just from watching all the different horses and riders."

"Oh, sure I have," answered Stevie, taking a long drink of water. "It's been great, but I can't help thinking that if Carole had been able to ride Starlight in these events, we'd be cheering for her instead of that girl from Texas."

"Well, that's true," Lisa agreed sadly.

Suddenly the stadium erupted in shouts. The Texas rider had ridden the course perfectly, her horse bounding over the jumps as lightly as a feather. The Saddle Club stood up and cheered as well. They knew when someone had done an exquisite job of riding and had earned a round of applause. As they watched, the horse and rider from Texas rode to the center of the ring and collected a blue ribbon and silver tray from the judge. Waving to the crowd, the girl rode a victory lap around the arena, a big grin on her face.

"She did a wonderful job!" exclaimed Carole. "I'm going to try a few of her tricks on Starlight the next time I ride him."

"Wonder when that will be?" said Stevie as they jumped from bleacher to bleacher, heading for the ground.

"Oh, maybe by next Christmas," Carole sighed. "If I'm lucky."

They joined the crowd that was slowly moving toward the gate. "Gee," said Lisa. "It's only two o'clock in the afternoon, and everything's over."

94

"That's right." Stevie shouldered her backpack and sighed, too. "No horses to look after, and no events to practice for. There's absolutely no point in staying here at Ashford Farms. What shall we do?"

"Knott's Berry Farm?" suggested Lisa. "Disneyland?"

Carole shook her head. "Since we've already been watching horses all day, why don't we go over and see how things are going for Skye?"

"How will we get there?" asked Stevie.

"I don't know," said Carole. "It's a two-mile walk, which is too long to do in riding boots. I guess we could call a cab."

"I don't think we're going to have to," said Lisa, peering into the parking lot just beyond the gate. "Isn't that Stephan, standing beside that big black limo? And isn't he motioning to us?"

"It sure is!" cried Stevie, waving back. "Looks like Skye had exactly the same idea we did."

Stephan drove them to the set, where Jess was waiting for them, their guest passes in hand.

"Hi, girls," he said worriedly. "I'm really glad Stephan found you."

"Stephan said Skye needed us." Carole frowned with concern. "What's going on?"

"You've been on a movie set before, haven't you?" Jess asked as he led them over to the barn.

"Yes," Stevie replied.

"Then you know that often we shoot out of sequence—sometimes scenes that are at the end of the movie are shot the first day of production."

"And?" Lisa asked, hurrying along behind Jess.

"And today Skye's shooting one of the final scenes—where his character, C.G., and Mabel have created a really close bond. The same close bond that will enable them to win the big race, which is being shot tomorrow."

"Is it a difficult scene?" asked Carole.

"It shouldn't be," replied Jess. "All Skye has to do is put her on a lead, take her to a place where he can put on her tack, and then tack her up. With all the stagehands we have handing him stuff off-camera, the whole thing should take about five minutes."

Jess stopped as they neared the big lights and cameras. "The only problem is Mabel. She's been nuts all day. Nothing Skye does seems to help, and George, the trainer, just makes it worse."

"Quiet on the set!" a loud voice called in their direction. They all turned. Shev Bayliss was scowling at them from behind a camera.

"Sorry, Shev," explained Jess. "These are Skye's guests. We didn't know you were ready to shoot."

"Well, we are," Shev growled. He stared angrily at the girls for another moment, then spoke again. "Take them over to those seats behind camera two," he snarled. "And make sure they keep their mouths shut."

Embarrassed by Shev's rudeness, Jess shrugged at the girls, then led them over to a row of seats behind one of the huge cameras. From there they could immediately see that everything was going wrong. George Gamble had just slammed Mabel's stall door shut, and Marcella was leading horse after horse in front of the stall. Mabel's ears were slapped back, and she was tossing her head in an angry, nervous way. Skye was talking to her and trying to calm her down, but nothing seemed to be doing any good.

"That horse is going to be a basket case by the time they start shooting," whispered Stevie.

"That horse is a basket case right now," said Carole. "So is Skye. And they haven't even begun to roll the film!"

Shev turned toward them and held up one finger.

"We'd better be quiet," whispered Lisa, "or he's going to throw us off the set."

"Okay, everybody, are we ready?" called a tall blond man who they assumed was the main director.

"The horse is," replied George. "I'm not so sure about our star."

"I'm ready." Skye looked over and smiled at the girls, but he looked almost as edgy as Mabel did.

"Okay," the director called. "Scene fifty-six. Take one. Action!"

The cameras rolled. Skye moved slowly toward Mabel, lead rope in hand. "Hi, girl," he began, reciting his lines. "Are you ready to show them what you can do?"

"Cut!" The director's voice roared over the set. "Try it again. The horse was looking the other way."

"You really need to get her attention, Skye," George called. "She's not one of your little fans that you can just flutter your eyelashes at."

Skye backed up to his mark, ready to try again.

"Okay, folks. Scene fifty-six. Take two," called the director. "Action!"

Again Skye stepped forward, holding the lead. "Hi, girl," he said. "Are you ready to show them what you can do?"

This time Mabel looked at him with soulful brown eyes, but when he moved to clip the lead on her halter, she slapped her ears back and bared her teeth.

"Cut!" the director snapped again.

"Ransom, you're coming at her too hard. She's going to bite you every time!" yelled George.

The Saddle Club looked at each other. Skye had done nothing that would make Mabel bite. In fact, he had clipped a lead rope on Mabel exactly the same way just the day before. Something weird was going on.

They turned their attention back to the set, where take three was about to begin. Everything went well, except the director yelled "Cut!" when Mabel tossed her head at the very moment Skye snapped her lead on.

Take four was cut when Mabel gave a loud snort just as Skye was delivering his lines.

On take five, Mabel kicked the stall, and by the time the director yelled "Cut!" on take six, everybody on the set was a nervous wreck.

"I don't know what's the matter with you people!" the director screamed at Skye and the rest of the crew. "This is the simplest scene in the movie. Boy greets horse, boy clips a lead line on her, boy saddles her up. If he's going to ride her to victory the next day, that should not be a problem!"

Skye began to say something when the director turned to George.

"What's your advice here, George? You're in charge of these creatures."

"Take a break," said George, shooting a look of disgust at Skye. "The horse needs to calm down. Ransom's upset her too much to go on."

"Take a break?" The director looked at George in disbelief. "Do you know how much it costs per day to film a movie?"

George shrugged. "I warned you and the producers. This is what happens when you put inexperienced actors together with high-strung horses."

"Okay, okay." The director shook his head. "I

guess you're right. Take ten, everybody! And come back ready to do this in one take!"

Suddenly everybody disappeared. Cameramen, sound people, assistants, and set decorators all scurried back to their trailers. Skye threw his lead line down on the ground and stalked off to a far corner of the stable.

"Come on," said Lisa. "Let's go talk to Skye. He looks like he could use some friends."

"Good idea." Carole bounded out of her chair. She was halfway across the set when she looked back at Stevie, who hadn't moved.

"Aren't you coming, Stevie?" she called.

"You go ahead," said Stevie. "I'll catch up with you guys later."

"Okay." Carole glanced once at Stevie, then she hurried over to an empty stall far away from Mabel, where Lisa was talking to Skye.

"I may not be a genius when it comes to horses," he was saying, angrily kicking a bale of hay. "But I do know a little bit about them. And I know that none of this is my fault!"

"That's absolutely right, Skye," said Carole. "None of this is your fault. Everybody has done everything they can to make that poor animal crazy!"

"That's true," said Lisa. "First George jerks her around, then they parade all those horses in front of her. No horse should be treated that way, especially when it's expected to be calm for a camera!"

"I know." Skye's face reddened with helpless anger. "But what can I do about it? How am I going to get through this film?"

"I don't know," said Lisa, giving a big sigh. "But I promise, we'll come up with something!"

Just then a whistle blew. The director was ready to start filming again.

"Here we go again," Skye said dejectedly, walking back to his mark by Mabel's stall. "Wish me luck."

Carole and Lisa gave him a thumbs-up, then returned to their seats beside Stevie.

"What happened to you?" Lisa asked as she sat down, noticing an impish grin on Stevie's face. "Skye really needed to talk."

"Oh, I figured you guys could cheer him up," Stevie replied mysteriously. "I worked my magic in other ways."

"Huh?" Carole frowned and started to ask Stevie what she meant, but another thunderous *Quiet!* from Shev made them all sit still and pay attention to the filming, which was about to begin.

"Okay, everybody," the director called. "Scene fifty-six. Take seven. Action!"

Skye moved forward, just as he had on the previous

six takes. "Hi, girl," he said. "Are you ready to show them what you can do?"

Mabel looked at him adoringly, her big eyes calm, her ears pricked and happy. Everyone on the set held their breath as Skye clipped the lead on her halter and led her out of the stall. Obedient as any horse at Pine Hollow, she didn't balk as the camera followed them to the paddock, and she stood absolutely still while Skye tacked her up. The Saddle Club kept their fingers crossed as he adjusted the saddle on her back and secured the stirrup leathers.

"Cut!" the director crowed. Everyone held their breath. Then, when he said, "And print!" everyone clapped with relief. Take seven was a success!

The director turned to the crew and smiled. "Nice work, everybody. And thanks especially to you, George. You really knew when to let that horse have a break."

George grinned at Shev as the crew moved on to shoot the next scene. The Saddle Club hurried over to Skye.

"Skye," said Lisa, "that was great!"

"Let's go back to my trailer," said Skye. "We can talk."

They all followed him to his trailer without saying a word. After they'd flopped down on his comfortable couch, Skye shut the door and turned to face them.

"Okay, Stevie," said Skye. "You stayed on the set

during the break. Tell me: What on earth did George Gamble do to calm that horse down?"

"Yes, Stevie," agreed Carole. "That's a good question. What did he do?"

"Who said George did anything?" Stevie looked at them with a sly smile. "The last I saw of George, he was heading for the caterer's trailer."

Lisa, Carole, and Skye stared at Stevie. "So what happened?"

"Well, I just went up to Mabel and had a little talk with her."

"A little talk made Mabel see the light of day?" Lisa looked doubtful.

"Well, maybe the little piece of apple I gave her," Stevie admitted.

"A little piece of apple?" Carole frowned.

"Well, maybe it was the little piece of tranquilizer I put inside the little piece of apple," Stevie confessed. "That might have had something to do with it."

"Tranquilizer?" Carole's brown eyes grew wide. "Stevie Lake, where did you get a horse tranquilizer?"

"Remember those pills Veronica gave me for Danny? Well, I put them in my backpack way back in Virginia. I found them again when I pulled out my water bottle at the Pony Club competition this afternoon." Stevie grinned. "I thought that if ever there was a time for some unauthorized drugging of a racehorse, this was it!"

"Oh, Stevie, I love you!" Skye rushed across the room and gave Stevie a gigantic hug. "Even if everybody on the set thinks I'm a jerk and George is a genius, I don't care. Thanks to you, I'm a much better actor, and I'm one scene closer to finishing this move!"

"Great!" Stevie returned Skye's hug, then she dug in her backpack on the floor. "Why don't you take the rest of the pills? If things get really bad again, you can give Mabel a little piece of one to calm her down. You'll have far more use for them with her than Veronica ever will with Danny."

"Could I?" Skye looked at the small bottle of green pills in his hand as if they were solid gold. "These will be great for the rest of our one-on-one scenes, but I don't know that they'll help for the big race scene. I can't ride her if she's drugged. She'll lose to the slowest of the other horses!"

Lisa frowned. "What are you going to do, then?"

"I don't know." Skye shook his head.

"I do," said Stevie. "Let's just rewrite the movie. We could have George be the evil trainer who bets against his racehorse and then drugs her so she'll lose the race!"

"Oh, Stevie!" Carole laughed and threw one of Skye's pillows at Stevie. Lisa joined in. Suddenly they were both pummeling her unmercifully.

"Wait, guys!" Laughing, Skye held up his hand. "I

cannot allow you to treat my new best friend Stevie Lake in such an undignified manner. She saved my job, at least for today, and she's helped The Saddle Club live up to its reputation!"

Giggling, Lisa and Carole started throwing pillows at Skye. Soon everybody was on the floor in the middle of a raucous pillow fight. They didn't stop until they heard a sharp rap at the door.

"Five minutes, Mr. Ransom," called a voice. "Scene forty-five."

"Oh, wow," Skye sighed, sitting in the middle of the floor. "Guess I've got to go back to work. Do you guys want to stay longer, or should Stephan drive you back to the hotel?"

"I think we'd better get back," said Lisa. "Max and Deborah might wonder where we are."

"Is there any chance you could come watch us tomorrow at the rally?" asked Carole. "Stevie and Lisa are supposed to compete."

"Yeah," said Stevie. "You could come cheer us on."

"I'd love to," Skye replied sadly. "But I can't. Tomorrow we're supposed to shoot the big race scene." He sighed again. "Believe me, I'd much rather come and watch you ride than try to ride Mabel, but duty calls."

"We understand," said Lisa. "Good luck, though."

"Yes, Skye," Stevie said. "Good luck."

"Thanks," he replied. "I'm sure I'll need it!"

# 10

"STEVIE? CAROLE? LISA? Wake up. I need to talk to you!"

Stevie's eyelids fluttered open. For a moment she didn't know where she was—all the familiar junk that surrounded her bed at home was missing. Then she sat up and looked around the room. Carole and Lisa were sleeping on the bed beside hers, while golden California sunshine streamed through the window.

Someone was knocking on their door.

"Just a minute!" Stevie called as she jumped out of bed. Without bothering to throw a robe over her huge University of Virginia sweatshirt, she pulled the door open. Deborah stood there, Maxi grinning from her arms.

"Hi." Stevie blinked sleepily. "What's going on?"

"I wanted to tell you that I just heard from the shipping company and they've guaranteed that your horses will be at Ashford Farms before noon."

"Really?" The thought of Belle woke Stevie up immediately. "That's wonderful!"

"I know," agreed Deborah with a smile. "Since you and Lisa are both scheduled to ride, you'd better get up and get ready. After all, that's what this trip was for, wasn't it?"

"Oh, absolutely," said Stevie.

"Well, why don't you wake Veronica up, too. Then you four can meet Max and me downstairs for breakfast in about twenty minutes. We can all ride to Ashford Farms in the rental car."

"Okay," Stevie replied. "That sounds great."

Deborah dubiously lifted one eyebrow. "You won't go back to sleep, will you?"

"Not now," promised Stevie. "I'm wide awake!"

"Okay, then. Twenty minutes."

With Maxi waving chubby fingers in farewell, Deborah hopped on the elevator while Stevie turned to wake her friends.

"Wake up, guys," Stevie called, pulling the blanket off Carole and Lisa. "Our horses are arriving sometime between now and noon. We've got to get ready to ride!"

Carole and Lisa sat up and rubbed their eyes. "They're actually bringing our horses?" asked Lisa. "How do you know?"

"Deborah just told me," said Stevie, hurrying into the bathroom to brush her teeth. "We're supposed to meet her and Max in twenty minutes for breakfast and then go over to Ashford Farms."

"Cool." Lisa sprang out of bed. "I'm so excited!"

"I'm excited, too," Carole said. "Or at least I'm excited that at least some of us will get to compete."

"It's really too bad about Starlight, Carole," said Stevie through a mouthful of toothpaste. "I know you could have won that hunter-jumper class."

"Well, maybe." Carole stretched her arms high above her head. "I did appreciate you guys being there for me, even when I didn't ride. I'll be happy to do the same for you today." She laughed. "You can just call me your equipment manager."

"That would be great," said Lisa. "If only we had some equipment for you to manage. Too bad it's still on the truck."

Everyone dressed quickly, with minutes to spare. "Let's hurry down to the dining room," said Carole. "For some reason, I'm starved!"

"Wait." Stevie frowned. "First we've got to wake Veronica."

They walked to the door that connected their

rooms and knocked loudly. They heard nothing, then the door jerked open.

"Yes?" Veronica was dressed in a frilly pink nightgown and had a white satin eye mask pushed up on her forehead.

"Hi, Veronica." For a moment Stevie could only blink at Veronica's weird sleeping attire. "Are you feeling better?"

Veronica looked at them strangely. "Why, yes. I feel fine."

"We're so sorry the sweetbreads didn't agree with you," Lisa said sympathetically.

"The sweetbreads?" Veronica frowned. "Why, it wasn't the sweetbreads at all. The doctor said I contracted a case of a rare stomach flu that only affects people with delicate constitutions."

"Well, would you like to bring your delicate constitution down to the dining room and have breakfast with the rest of us?" Stevie asked. "Our horses are supposed to arrive before noon, and we're all going over to Ashford Farms to wait for them."

Veronica gave a haughty snort. "What would be the point in that? I'm not scheduled to ride Danny in anything. I'd just be stuck there watching you guys and a bunch of other amateurs who have nothing to teach me." She removed the mask from her forehead and shook her dark hair. "I'm going to get a cab and go shopping. I can't imagine wasting a perfectly good trip to Los Angeles without stopping at least once on Rodeo Drive. I'll see you people at dinner tonight."

With a toss of her head, Veronica closed her door. Stevie, Carole, and Lisa just looked at each other.

"Well," said Lisa. "Guess the stomach flu didn't improve her delicate constitution very much."

"Oh, look on the bright side," Stevie said with a grin. "We've never had an easier time getting rid of Veronica diAngelo, and we didn't have to do a thing!"

They hurried down to the hotel café, where Max, Deborah, and Maxi were waiting for them. This time, Stevie ordered scrambled eggs and bacon instead of her new yogurt-and-jam concoction.

"You don't have the stomach flu, too, do you?" Lisa asked, glancing at Stevie's normal-looking plate.

"Oh, no." Stevie chomped her bacon happily as she buttered a piece of toast for Maxi to gnaw. "I'm just too excited about seeing Belle to invent any new breakfasts today."

"That's a relief." Carole laughed. "We get worried when you start to eat like a regular person."

They finished breakfast quickly, then they all piled into the rental car and drove to Ashford Farms. Cars and horse trailers were parked alongside the long driveway, and inside the showgrounds it looked as if every Pony Club member in the world was waiting to ride. People had already crowded into the arena, and outside even more were milling around the different exhibits and rides and refreshment stands.

"Everybody, look and see if we can find the In-Transit van with our horses!" Stevie cried, bolting upright in the backseat.

"Good idea," said Carole. They all searched for the big red van as Max parked the car, but nobody spotted it.

"Don't worry yet," said Deborah, hoisting Maxi on one hip as they began to walk back toward the arena. "They aren't due until noon. And I made them promise to page us from the ring announcer's stand when they got here."

"Do you think they know what *page* means?" asked Stevie.

Deborah shrugged. "Let's hope."

"Why don't we just concentrate on having fun until they come," suggested Max. "It'll keep us all from getting nervous."

"Sounds like a good idea to me," said Carole. She looked over at the pony ride, which had just stopped to let new passengers on. "May I take Maxi on that pony ride?"

"Sure," laughed Deborah, who was having trouble holding the squirming Maxi. "In fact, I think that's exactly what she wants to do."

Carole scooped up Maxi and carried her over to

the pony ride. She placed her on a fat little pinto pony and held on to her while the pony walked slowly around the ring. Maxi squealed in delight, and Max filmed her with his video camera.

"Poooo-neeee," she gurgled, holding on to the little horse's thick mane. "Poooo-neeee!"

Though everyone laughed as Carole and Maxi walked around the ring, Stevie and Lisa kept looking over their shoulders, watching for the big red van to pull up. By the time Maxi had ridden the pony ride five times, it still hadn't shown up.

"Let's go look at those exhibits on the other side of the arena," said Lisa as Carole gave Maxi back to Deborah.

"What time is it?" asked Stevie, again looking for the van.

Carole glanced at her watch. "Ten-thirty. They've still got an hour and a half to get here."

"Okay," Stevie said. "We might as well educate ourselves while we wait."

They walked to the other side of the arena, where a number of booths had been set up. One displayed a new line of tack made specifically for jumping and dressage, while another exhibited barn mats constructed to massage horses' hooves with tiny magnets. The girls looked at feed booths and boot booths and finally a book booth that specialized in novels about horses. All the while they kept looking over their shoulders, hoping to see the big red van.

"What time is it now?" asked Stevie as they came to the end of the booths.

"Eleven-thirty," reported Carole.

Stevie looked at her friends, her hazel eyes wide. "They've got thirty minutes to get here!"

"Maybe they ran into traffic," said Carole.

"Look, they could get here as late as one o'clock and we could still ride," reasoned Lisa. "Our event doesn't start until two."

"That's cutting it awfully close," said Stevie.

"Yes, but it still gives them an hour and a half to arrive," said Lisa. "Let's go get something to eat. That way we'll be ready to go when they come."

They walked over to a refreshment stand, where they got two hot dogs apiece. When they'd finished those, they watched a training seminar on how to get reluctant horses to cross a stream calmly. Though the seminar was interesting, each of the girls still kept looking for the red van and listening for their names to be called on the PA system.

"What time is it now?" whispered Stevie.

Carole looked at her watch and shuddered. "Twelve-thirty."

"Let's go find Max and Deborah," suggested Lisa.

They left the seminar and began searching for the

Regnerys. It took them a while to locate them in the stands, but finally they found them. Deborah was holding Maxi while Max watched a hunter-jumper class.

"Hi." Deborah looked up at them. The look on her face told them everything.

"Nobody's showed up yet, have they?" Stevie asked.

Deborah shook her head. "What time is it?"

"Twelve-forty-five," Carole said sadly.

"Let me call them again." Deborah handed Maxi to Lisa while she dug her cell phone out of her purse. Punching in the number that she now knew by heart, she held the phone to her ear and waited. The phone rang many times, but no one answered. She looked at the girls and shook her head.

"Nobody at the shipping company," she reported. "Let me try the driver's cell phone."

This time she had to check a number she'd scribbled in her day planner. Once again, the phone rang many times, but no one picked up. Shaking her head, she clicked the phone off and looked at the girls.

"I'm sorry," Deborah said. "But nobody's there, either."

"What?" cried Stevie, her face red with anger. "How can nobody be there? How can they promise they'll have our horses here and then just not show up? It's too late now. Even if they came right this instant we wouldn't have enough time to get ready!"

"That's right," said Lisa. "We've spent a lot of time and money to come out here and compete. Thanks to this stupid van company, this whole trip is turning out to be a big zero!"

"I'm sorry, girls," said Max. "I've used this company before and they've never been incompetent." He shook his head in frustration. "I'm sure they'll adjust our shipping bill, so we'll get some of our money back."

"Adjust it like how much?" asked Stevie.

"Like down to nothing, if he has anything to say about it." Deborah looked at Max.

Max frowned. "Look, there's nothing we can do about this now. Why don't you guys come to Disneyland with us? That way you can at least have a little fun on your last afternoon in California."

The girls looked at each other. Each knew that if they couldn't be there riding, there was only one other place they wanted to be.

"No," said Stevie. "Thanks. That sounds like fun, but since we can't ride, we need to go and cheer for someone who can."

Max smiled. "Would that someone be Skye Ransom?"

The girls nodded. "He's shooting his big racing scene today," Lisa explained.

"Well, would you like a lift over to Ashford Race-track since we're going in that direction?"

"That would be great, Max," said Carole, taking Maxi from Deborah's arms.

"Yes," laughed Stevie. "Since for once we don't have Stephan waiting."

They left the arena and hurried back to the car. They still kept looking for a big red van to pull up in a cloud of dust, but no new horses or riders were arriving. In fact, more people were leaving than arriving as Max pulled into the line of traffic on the highway.

"Now, you guys know we have to be at the airport by seven in the morning, don't you?" he asked, glancing at them in the rearview mirror.

"Right," said Lisa.

"Then why don't we agree to meet back at the hotel by six this evening. We'll have an early dinner and get a good night's sleep."

"Okay, Max," agreed Carole as their car pulled into the Ashford Racetrack driveway. "That won't be a problem."

"All right, then," Max called as they got out of the car. "We'll see you girls around six."

"Bye!" called Stevie.

"Have fun," Deborah replied. "Good luck to Skye!"

Since their names were already on the studio guest

list, they had no trouble getting past security. They headed for Skye's trailer.

"I hope we're not too late," said Stevie.

"I know," Lisa agreed. "Skye would feel so much better if we were here, watching him while he worked."

"Let's hurry," said Carole.

They made their way to Skye's trailer and knocked softly on the door, which opened immediately. Jess Morton stood there, a worried frown on his face.

"Oh boy," he said. "Am I glad to see you three!"

"What's the matter?" asked Carole. "You look upset."

"It's just been an awful morning," explained Jess. "Skye's a wreck. He's had calls from three different gossip columnists who wanted to confirm a rumor they'd heard that he'd been fired from the movie and Fred Gamble was taking his place!"

"Who told them that?" cried Lisa.

Jess shrugged. "An unnamed source, according to them. You can imagine how that made Skye feel."

"Where's he now?" asked Stevie.

"Down on the set. They're getting ready to shoot his big scene."

"Are we in time to watch?" asked Carole.

"Absolutely!" said Jess, hustling them back down the trailer steps. "In fact, I'd say you guys got here just in time to help. Let's go!"

THE SADDLE CLUB hurried along behind Jess, arriving at the racetrack just as the scene was about to begin. In the movie, the action was to take place on a windy, rainy day, so along with the huge klieg lights and microphones were other movie effect machines that produced sheets of rain and gusts of blustery wind.

The girls easily picked Mabel out from the crowd of horses milling around the starting gate. She was already dancing away from the man who held her, her ears slapped back and a wild look in her eyes. Skye, who was sitting in his own special chair, didn't look much better. Though he wore movie makeup and his green-and-white jockey silks costume, the girls saw that his mouth was pulled down in a tight, nervous line, and his twinkling blue eyes were clouded with concern.

"Sit right here," Jess whispered, leading them to a long bench just behind a camera. "And don't make a sound!"

The girls nodded, then watched as the director strutted out to the middle of the set, grinning as if everything were perfectly all right.

"Okay, people," he called, addressing everyone. "After yesterday's success, I know this race scene is going to be great. It's not going to be easy, but we have a great cast and crew, and I'm confident that Skye can work with this magnificent horse and get the best performance out of her possible." He paused for a moment, then smiled again. "Is everybody ready?"

Everyone concerned—except Skye—either mumbled yes or nodded.

"Okay, then," the director said. "Let's get rolling."

Mabel's groom hauled her, kicking and balking, closer to Skye. Her white face had been washed almost to a glow, and her dark bay coat shone with a deep luster.

"She's so pretty," whispered Lisa. "She reminds me of—"

"Shhh!" said Carole. "Be quiet or they'll make us leave!"

While the groom held on to Mabel, another handler tried to put her saddle on. First she shied away. Then she reared. The third time she tried to bite the groom. Two more grooms were called in to help hold her head. Finally, after ten more minutes of twisting and fighting, they buckled a tiny racing saddle on the frantic horse.

"I would call Mabel more monstrous than magnificent," whispered Stevie, frowning as Skye rose from his chair and slowly walked toward the horse.

"Okay, Skye," said the director. "Are you ready?"

Skye nodded, though he looked ashen beneath his makeup. With one groom holding Mabel's head, he put his left foot in the stirrup and tried to swing up. Immediately, Mabel whirled around to the left, her massive hindquarters knocking Skye to the ground. Carole, Lisa, and Stevie all winced. They knew how much that could hurt. To their amazement, a snicker floated up from behind the director. They turned. George, Shev Bayliss, and Marcella all had sarcastic smiles on their faces.

"How mean can these people be?" cried Lisa.

"Shhh!" said Stevie. "Skye's going to try again."

The groom held Mabel tighter as Skye tried a second time. This time Mabel stood calmly until he was almost sitting in the saddle, then she jumped and twisted at the same time. Skye bounced once on Mabel's back, then thudded to the ground again.

"This is awful!" cried Carole. "This horse is not fit to be ridden, much less star in the movies!"

"Skye has a lot of guts to do this," said Stevie.

They watched as Skye tried to mount Mabel for the third time. This time the other groom came over and held the saddle to keep Mabel steady. The two grooms were able to hold the horse still enough for Skye to finally put both feet in the short racing stirrups.

"Bravo!" shouted George, clapping his hands loudly. "He actually mounted the horse! What a performance!"

Mabel jumped once at the sound of hands clapping, but Skye managed to hold her still.

"Okay," said the director. "Let's get her into the starting gate."

With Skye perched on Mabel's back, the grooms began to lead her down the track. She took about three strides, then began to walk sideways. When Skye and the grooms tried to straighten her out, she lunged at one groom, then tried to bite the other. As the man jumped away from her snapping teeth, he let go of her bridle. Mabel saw her chance. In a flash she turned from racehorse to bucking bronco, twisting and turning and finally rearing high into the air. Skye hung on the whole time, desperately trying to rein the horse away from the terrified crew members and the expensive movie equipment.

"Somebody grab that horse!" shouted the director. "She's going to kill somebody!"

The grooms ran after her, grabbing at her bridle. After a few more moments of bucking and snorting, Mabel finally calmed down enough to allow them to seize her bridle. Skye remained in the saddle the whole time, ready to rein Mabel in again should she take off once more.

"Okay, Skye," the director called disappointedly. "Jump down and take ten. Something's definitely wrong here. George, come on over here. We need to talk."

The girls watched as Skye dismounted and strode over to where George and the director were conferring. Another tall, skinny bald man joined the group from the other side of the set.

"Who's that?" asked Lisa, watching as the four men began talking at once.

"I don't know," Stevie replied. "But be quiet and maybe we can hear what they're saying."

"What's wrong with this movie is Ransom!" the girls heard George say angrily. "He's just not the horseman he guaranteed us he was!"

"Now hold on," said the skinny bald man. "I'm Jim Young, Skye's agent. I've heard all the rumors that have been flying around this set. Let me remind you two that Skye Ransom has ridden horses very successfully in five feature films and half a dozen television

dramas. Nobody has ever complained about his ability to ride!" He glared at George. "I think somebody
sold you a bill of goods on this horse!"

"That's baloney!" George snapped, grabbing Mabel's reins. "This horse has been in more movies than
Ransom, and she's carried her riders perfectly! I'm not
going to stand here and listen to this malarkey!

"Come on, Mabel!" he cried, tugging the horse
back toward the barn. "You need to get away from
these movie stars who just *think* they can ride horses!"

George sneered at Skye, then led Mabel back to
her stall. Everyone else on the set milled around
as Skye and the other two men conferred, waiting to
see what would happen. Carole and Lisa were observ-
ing Skye intently when Stevie poked them in the
ribs.

"Look!" Stevie whispered.

"Be quiet, Stevie!" Carole replied. "This is important. This might ruin Skye's career!"

"I know, but look anyway." Stevie pointed to the
other side of the track, where a vaguely familiar red
horse van had just lumbered up.

"So?" Carole said. "It's a horse van. There are
about fifty more parked behind the stable."

"No, really look," Stevie insisted. "Look again at
the name on the side."

Carole and Lisa squinted their eyes. "Good grief!"
Lisa cried. "That's the In-Transit van!"

"Those are our horses!" Carole's dark eyes danced with joy.

They jumped up from the bench and ran across the track to the trailer. They reached the van just as the driver climbed out of the cab. He looked at all the cameras and lights, then scratched his head. "Is this Ashford Farms?" he asked as the girls ran up beside him.

Before anyone could say a word, another voice rang out from behind them.

"Thank heavens!" a woman's voice cried. "I knew we were going to need some extra horses. How wonderful you delivered them so promptly."

The girls turned. Marcella stood there, beaming at the van driver.

"You need to drive these horses up to that barn, now." She pointed to one of the track barns. "Just put them in whatever stalls you find available."

"Yes, ma'am," the driver said as he climbed back in the cab.

"But wait—" Stevie began.

"Come on, Stevie," said Carole. "Let's just follow him and see if these really are our horses."

While the driver restarted the big truck, the girls cut across two training paddocks, running as fast as they could. They reached the stable just as the driver pulled up.

"Didn't I just see you three over there?" he asked as he climbed out of the cab.

"Yes," said Stevie. "They sent us over here to help you unload the horses."

"Whatever," said the driver. He unlocked the huge doors at the back of the trailer and pulled out the ramp. The girls hurried inside. There, looking out from their traveling stalls, stood Belle and Starlight and Prancer and Danny.

"I don't believe it!" Tears rimmed Stevie's eyes as she gave Belle a big hug. "I didn't think I'd ever see you again."

"Don't they look great?" Carole rubbed Starlight behind the ears and gave Danny a pat on the nose.

"They sure do," agreed Lisa, brushing a piece of hay off Prancer's white face. "I feel like they've been gone for years!"

The driver stuck his head in the door and asked, "Do you girls know where these horses are supposed to go?"

Stevie, Lisa, and Carole looked at each other and started to laugh. "Actually, we do," said Carole. "We may be the only people in America who know exactly where these horses are supposed to go."

"Well, who's supposed to sign for them?" The driver held up a clipboard. "I can't unload them until I get a signature."

"I'll sign for them." Carole stepped to the back of the truck and scribbled her name across the form. *Carole Hanson*, she wrote proudly. *Pine Hollow Stables, Willow Creek, Virginia.*

A few minutes later, they had all the horses unloaded and settled into stalls. They seemed to be in good shape, although Danny looked tired and Starlight looked eager to stretch his legs in a big paddock. Belle was her usual playful self and tried to take a delicate nibble of Stevie's hair.

"Ow!" giggled Stevie as Belle's soft mouth grazed the back of her neck. "I think listening to Mozart all the way across the country really did make Belle smarter. She now thinks she can eat my hair when I'm not looking!"

"It didn't seem to affect Prancer much one way or the other," said Lisa, smiling as Prancer stood calmly in the stall next to Mabel's. The movie horse was still kicking and trying to rear. "I guess racehorses get accustomed to being hauled around the country and it just doesn't bother them anymore."

"That's right," said Carole. "I keep forgetting that Prancer was a racehorse when she was younger. She's so calm and untemperamental—unlike most racehorses."

"She's a great horse, whatever she was," said Lisa. She reached up to hug Prancer around her neck when the stall beside her shuddered. Lisa looked next door.

Mabel had given the wall a mighty kick and was glaring at Lisa, her ears slapped back on her head. Lisa frowned at the misbehaving mare, then she stepped back. *Hmmm*, she thought, an idea suddenly occurring to her.

"Hey, Stevie, Carole—come over here," she said. "Come have a look at this."

Stevie and Carole came and stood beside Lisa. "Good grief!" cried Stevie. "Why didn't any of us see that before?"

# 12

STEVIE, CAROLE, AND Lisa were sitting back on their bench by the time the director was ready to shoot the scene again. Though Skye was pacing beside his chair, looking worriedly at the ground, they all sat calmly, big grins on their faces.

"Okay, everybody, places!" the director called through a small bullhorn.

The lighting crew and cameramen scrambled for their equipment. Everyone held their breath as George led Mabel down from the stable, clearly expecting the horse to behave just as badly as she had before. Instead of being skittish and troubled, though, Mabel now walked as meekly as a lamb, following George agreeably despite his hard tugs on her lead. Everyone on the set gasped in disbelief, and even

George looked around more than once, surprised at Mabel's sudden change in behavior.

"Oh boy," whispered Stevie, nudging Lisa and Carole. "This is going to be good."

George led Mabel back to the middle of the track, then turned to Skye. "You want to see if you can saddle her now, Ransom?" he asked, his voice sneering. "Or should I call for some help?"

"That's okay," Skye replied, trying to sound confident. "I'm sure Mabel and I will be fine." With a deep breath, he picked up the tiny racing saddle and walked slowly toward the horse, George glaring at him the whole time.

"Hey, girl," Skye said softly, remembering to approach Mabel with his eyes lowered, just as Carole had. He reached out a hand to touch her, expecting her to flinch, but Mabel stood calmly, seeming to enjoy Skye's hand on her neck. Gently, he put the saddle pad on her back, again expecting her to go crazy, but Mabel stood still. George began to cough, jerking the lead again in the process, but Mabel did not react. Skye put the saddle on her back and reached beneath her to tighten the girth. Amazingly, Mabel didn't move a muscle. Skye looked at George and smiled.

"Okay," sneered George. "So you saddled her up. Now let's see you get on her."

Skye buckled his jockey helmet, then grabbed the

reins and put one foot in the stirrup. At first he tightened his muscles, waiting for Mabel to either knock him to the ground or run away sideways, but again, she stood calm. When he hoisted himself up in the saddle and settled gently on her back, he once again prepared to be thrown to the ground. But it didn't happen. Mabel seemed to actually enjoy being in the middle of the racetrack with a rider on her back.

Everyone on the set began to applaud. "Nicely done, Skye," called the director. For the first time that day, the tension seemed to leave Skye's shoulders.

"Okay," growled George. "Now let's see if you can get her in the starting gate."

Skye took the reins firmly in both hands and squeezed his legs. He was obviously wondering if either of those aids would send Mabel into a buck or a rear or a flat-out run, but instead she just started walking easily in the direction Skye wanted her to go. Mabel didn't even protest about going into the narrow starting gate. She stepped gracefully into the small, tight space without a flick of her ears and stood calmly as the grooms shut the doors behind her.

Now grinning broadly, Skye looked over at The Saddle Club with a questioning gaze. All three just shrugged and then smiled as if they were three cats who'd just consumed three very delicious canaries.

130

"We did it!" cried Carole in a whisper. "We actually did it!"

"I know, but be quiet now," replied Lisa. "I want to watch them film this scene."

The girls settled down and watched as the other horses and riders were loaded into the gate around Mabel. Again, Mabel behaved beautifully, appearing almost eager for the gate to open so that she could fly down the track. The director climbed on the camera truck that would film the racing horses from the front as they ran.

"Okay, everybody, this is scene eighty-eight, take one. Remember, Skye is supposed to win, but I want horses number six and one to come in close as we enter the turn. Everybody got that?"

Skye and the stunt riders nodded.

"All right, then. Action on my mark!"

The director lifted his arm, paused for a moment, then dropped it to his waist. Cameras began rolling. The starting bell went off and the gates flew open. Eight horses thundered down the track, Mabel running easily in the lead. Carole, Stevie, and Lisa stood on the bench to watch the action around the first turn.

"How's Mabel doing?" Stevie asked, squinting in the bright sunlight.

"She's doing great!" cried Lisa. "I think she's ahead by two lengths!"

The horses roared around the backstretch, then crossed the finish line in a blur. The director yelled "Cut!" Again, everyone on the set applauded.

"Wonderful, Skye," the director said, running over to shake Skye's hand. "That was terrific!"

"This is the craziest horse!" cried Skye, giving Mabel a pat on the shoulder. "Inside the barn she's wild, but once you get her on the track, it's almost like she's come home. She runs like she really means it!"

"No kidding," gasped one of the stunt riders. "We couldn't catch you after the first furlong. You're going to have to pull her back if we're going to make this look like a race!"

The girls laughed and hugged each other on top of the bench, then they sat down quickly as George and Marcella stomped by.

"I don't understand what's happening," griped Marcella. "He didn't have a clue about that horse ten minutes ago."

"Don't worry," George said softly. "He'll mess up again, and it'll cost the producer big time. We just have to keep our eyes open and point it out when he does."

The Saddle Club watched as George, Marcella, and Shev walked over to sit right beside the starting gate, glaring at Skye the whole time.

"Can you believe that?" whispered Stevie. "They're still out to sabotage Skye."

"Yes, but they won't get the chance now," said Carole. "This should be as much fun to watch as the filming."

The next shot was of the horses coming around one of the curves. A camera truck drove right along-side the horses to film the action. George and Shev and Marcella stood up and watched Skye's riding like three evil hawks, but they could make no criticism. Skye rode beautifully, and Mabel ran as if she'd been a racehorse since the day she was born.

"That's a take!" the director called as Skye and Mabel again crossed the finish line. "Nice job, Skye! And somebody give that horse a carrot!"

Much to The Saddle Club's delight, George and Marcella just looked at each other and frowned.

The filming took the rest of the afternoon as the director insisted on multiple takes of the horses coming out of the starting gate, running down the stretch and through the turns. But Mabel and Skye made a great team. In fact, Mabel carried Skye across the finish line a dozen times without even a flick of her tail, and Skye grew more confident of his abilities with each take. Even the more experienced stunt riders congratulated Skye on his riding skill.

"I don't know what you did to that nag, but it sure

made a difference in her screen performance," said one stunt rider. "She was so nervous at the start, I thought we were going to have to carry both of you across that finish line!"

"I know." Skye laughed and gave Mabel a good scratch behind her ears. "Now she's so calm I'm afraid I might have to wake her up before the next shot!"

The last shot was scheduled just as the sun began to set behind the California mountains. The director explained what he wanted after all the horses were loaded in the starting gate.

"Okay, everybody. One more time around the track. This time we'll have a handheld camera right behind Skye to give the audience a real sense of what it's like to ride in a race. It'll be tricky, but if our luck and Mabel's good mood hold, we'll be done for the day. Everyone ready?"

The riders nodded, and the cameraman who was riding right beside them got ready to shoot.

"Okay, then." The director moved to the side of the track. "Action!"

The gates opened and the horses blazed out. Though Mabel should have been exhausted from the day's filming, she strode on like a true Thoroughbred, her long legs gobbling up the ground. Everyone watched as Skye and the cameraman rode together around the track, then when they crossed the finish line, the director yelled, "Cut! And print! Good job, everybody. See you at seven A.M. tomorrow in the studio for interiors!"

Almost everybody cheered as Skye pulled Mabel up and dismounted. Only three people sat frowning in silence—George, Marcella, and Shev. They got up from their perches beside the track and walked over to Skye and Mabel.

"Well, looks like you got lucky, Ransom," George said, grabbing Mabel's reins away from Skye. "No more scenes that require a real rider in this movie. You can just bat your eyelashes at the camera from here on out."

For a moment Skye looked angry, then he smiled and handed Mabel a lump of sugar. "Whatever, George," he said. "My only regret in this movie is that this poor horse has to be cared for by you."

George muttered something else, then he led Mabel back to the barn, the whole time shaking and jerking the lead line, trying to make her misbehave. Instead of jumping and biting, though, Mabel just followed calmly, nodding her head at some crew members along the way.

From their seats on the bench, The Saddle Club could see the whole thing. "Come on," said Lisa. "I want to find out what George is going to do next."

All three got up and followed George and Mabel, careful to stay far enough away to escape his notice. He jerked Mabel back to the barn, still failing to get a rise out of her. The longer he tried, the calmer she got and the redder his face became. By the time they reached her stall, he practically shoved the poor horse inside.

"Get in there!" he snapped, popping the end of the reins on Mabel's flank. As soon as she was safely in her stall, he slammed the door so hard the whole stable shook. Then, without ever noticing that the three visitors from Virginia were standing nearby, he stormed out of the stable, muttering something under his breath.

"Wow," whispered Stevie. "He's really mad!"

"I know," Carole replied. "I pity the poor horse that belongs to him."

"Can you believe we actually did this?" cried Lisa, her blue eyes alight with joy.

"No!" cried Stevie, lifting her hand in a high five. "I think this is one of the most amazing stunts we've ever pulled off! We should go down in the annals of Hollywood history!"

They all gave each other high fives in a small, tight circle. Mabel watched them curiously, then she whinnied as someone entered the stable. The girls stopped celebrating and turned around. Skye stood there, a big grin on his face.

"Hi," he said. "What's going on? Why do I have the feeling that The Saddle Club has just played a major part in that scene with Mabel and me?"

The girls looked at one another, each dying to tell Skye their big secret.

"Well, Skye, remember that pizza delivery boy who came to your trailer the other morning?" Stevie began.

## 13

"YOU WANT THE same thing you had last time?" The waitress at TD's frowned at Stevie.

"Right," Stevie replied with a smile. "Lime and orange sherbet, only this time with pistachio sauce instead of hot fudge and pecans instead of marshmallows."

"I get it," the waitress said as she wrote Stevie's order on her pad. "Just the same, only different."

"Well, I suppose," agreed Stevie.

"Kids!" the waitress muttered, shaking her head as she walked back to the soda fountain.

"Stevie, why did you change your order?" asked Lisa. "You haven't eaten pistachio sauce in months."

"I don't know," sighed Stevie. "For some reason, pistachios have a real California feel to them."

Carole and Lisa looked at each other. "You know," Carole said, "I can kind of see what she means."

"Didn't we have a great time in California?" said Lisa, spreading out the four blue ribbons they'd won on the table. "I miss being there so much."

"I do, too," said Stevie. "I miss Stephan driving us around in that cushy limo. Now I'm stuck in the backseat of our station wagon again, riding with my bratty brothers."

"I miss seeing all those wonderful horses at the Pony Club show," said Carole. "Some really terrific competitors rode there."

"I miss Skye," Lisa said. "And the expression on his face when we told him what we'd done."

"He did look pretty amazed, didn't he?" laughed Stevie. "He knew we'd done something, but I don't think he imagined in his wildest dreams that we'd switched Mabel and Prancer!"

"I don't think Prancer ever imagined in her wildest dreams that she'd be switched with a movie horse!" added Lisa with a chuckle.

"Yes, but did you see the look on her face?" asked Carole. "She's a retired racehorse, so it must have felt great to be back on the track, racing in front of a grandstand."

"I know she loved going in that starting gate," said Lisa. "I could tell that from where we were sitting."

"And George and Marcella and Shev never suspected a thing!" cackled Stevie. "That's the best part of all!"

"Skye said we really saved his career," Carole said. "I think he would have done anything to repay us for all our help."

"Yes, but we couldn't have taken that money he offered." Lisa smiled as the waitress brought their ice cream. "Friends can't take money from friends for helping out like that."

"He came up with a pretty great idea just the same," said Stevie as she dived into her sherbet sundae. "I mean, hiring a totally different first-class van service to get our horses back to Virginia in two days was really something!"

"I think he put Jess on the case," said Lisa. "Jess looked as worried about Skye as we were."

"Well, they're both great guys," Carole said. "Skye's career is zooming, Jess is happy, and we have our wonderful horses back home."

"And they look happy and very rested," added Lisa.

"Why shouldn't they be?" asked Stevie. "They never had to do anything except ride around in a trailer and listen to Mozart."

"That's right." Carole giggled. "We should be pretty rested, too. After we rode in that one competition, all we did was get chauffeured back and forth to a movie set."

Just then, TD's door jingled open and Veronica walked in. She was wearing leopard-print pants with a fluffy white sweater. Bright green earrings dangled from her ears, and her eyes were shaded by dark wrap-around sunglasses.

"Uh-oh," whispered Stevie as Veronica walked toward their table. "Here comes somebody who got more rest than anybody, thanks to her appetite for sweetbreads."

"Hi," Veronica said, giving them a thin smile. "How do you like my new outfit? I bought it on Rodeo Drive while you three were out pestering that poor Skye Ransom."

"It's great, Veronica," replied Stevie. "It looks like something you'd see in the movies—although I'm not sure which one."

"Here," Carole said, pushing one of the blue ribbons toward Veronica. "See if this will go with it."

"What's this for?" Veronica asked dubiously.

"Remember that morning you were too sick to ride? Well, Skye rode in your place in the mounted games. Thanks to him, we came in first. I guess the ribbon really belongs to him, but somehow it wound up back here in Virginia."

Veronica took the ribbon from Carole. "Thanks,"

she said. "I'm sure I would have won it anyway, if it hadn't been for that weird California water."

Without another word, she turned and sauntered out the door. The girls watched her, dumbfounded.

"I don't believe that!" cried Lisa.

"I don't either," Carole said. "She actually took a ribbon she didn't win!"

Stevie shrugged. "I don't know why you two are surprised. When has Veronica *not* taken credit for other people's work?"

"Well, I hadn't thought of it that way, but I guess you're right," said Carole.

"It doesn't matter," Stevie said. "We know who really won the race."

"Just like we really know which horse was the better actor," giggled Carole.

"That's true," Lisa agreed. "And part of what we learned this week is that substitution isn't always bad."

"Particularly when it's for an excellent cause," added Carole.

"I'll drink to that!" said Stevie, lifting her water glass high.

"And I'll drink to The Saddle Club," said Lisa. "Great friends to have in times of trouble, wherever you might be!"

## ABOUT THE AUTHOR

BONNIE BRYANT is the author of more than a hundred books about horses, including The Saddle Club series, The Saddle Club Super Editions, the Pony Tails series, and Pine Hollow, which follows the Saddle Club girls into their teens. She has also written novels and movie novelizations under her married name, B. B. Hiller.

Ms. Bryant began writing The Saddle Club in 1986. Although she had done some riding before that, she intensified her studies then and found herself learning right along with her characters Stevie, Carole, and Lisa. She claims that they are all much better riders than she is.

Ms. Bryant was born and raised in New York City. She still lives there, in Greenwich Village, with her two sons.

Don't miss the next exciting
Saddle Club adventure . . .

# MILLION-DOLLAR HORSE
## Saddle Club #92

Pine Hollow Stables has a new resident, and while The Saddle Club loves all horses, they aren't impressed by this one. Honey-Pie is a sweet old mare, but there's nothing special about her—or is there? It turns out that Honey-Pie is a million-dollar horse! She inherited her million from her owner, Emma Fredericks. Mrs. Fredericks also left a million dollars to her nephew, Paul, but his money's all gone. Now Paul wants Honey-Pie's inheritance, and he'll do anything to get it. It's up to The Saddle Club to save Honey-Pie and unmask Paul as the horse-hating rat that he is!

# MEET
# the SADDLE CLUB

Horse lover CAROLE . . .
Practical joker STEVIE . . .
Straight-A LISA . . .

# THE SADDLE CLUB
## SUPER EDITIONS

# THE SADDLE CLUB
## SPECIAL EDITIONS

**Stevie Lake is famous for her crazy schemes,
but now she's in trouble—
she needs a scheme that's *really* crazy!**

# Stevie: The Inside Story

Stevie Lake is in trouble. Big trouble. She's failing classes, and if she doesn't pull her grades up fast it means summer school and, worst of all, no riding. She has one last chance to redeem herself. She's got to write a report explaining why she hasn't done her homework or studied for the past few months—and she's got to make the explanation good. Stevie's serious. She's committed. She's going to get this assignment done if it kills her.

And of course her best friends want to help—and give their side of the story. By the time they're all finished with the encouraging e-mails, personal essays, and phone calls, Stevie will have more than an essay. She'll have a multimedia spectacular!

*Covers events in The Saddle Club books 20 through 22*

**Lisa Atwood is the calm member of
The Saddle Club, but now and then
even calm people need to vent!**

# Lisa: The Inside Story

Lisa Atwood tried keeping a diary once, but it wasn't a success. Why would she want to write in a book when she can tell her Saddle Club friends, Stevie Lake and Carole Hanson, everything? But then Lisa realizes that there are times when she needs a private place to record her thoughts. For example, why do people still call her a beginning rider when she's come such a long way? And why can't Stevie and Carole understand her desire to be the very best at everything she does, even school? And why is her mother always driving her crazy, trying to make her into a perfect lady? Sometimes even Lisa's best friends don't get how frustrating all that can be.

And then there are the good things, like the excitement Lisa feels when she masters a new riding skill or does well on a test. Those are memories she wants to keep forever. Maybe a diary is a good idea after all.

*Covers events in The Saddle Club books 23 through 29*

**Carole Hanson knows everything about horses, but sometimes she forgets the most important things.**

# Carole: The Inside Story

Carole Hanson knows she wants to spend her life with horses—the problem is, she doesn't know how. She could be a vet, or a professional rider, or she could run her own stable. She needs to narrow the choices down a bit, but it's hard. And there are so many other things she wants to do—including great Saddle Club projects like helping her friend Stevie choose a horse, helping her friend Marie get through a difficult birthday, and helping her friend Lisa fulfill her dream of going on the stage. It's a lot of work, but that's what The Saddle Club is all about: helping each other out. But who's going to help Carole with her decision?

Then her old riding journals and a special set of memories help Carole realize that she doesn't have to decide anything just yet.

*Covers events in The Saddle Club books 34 through 40*